"His room is starting to get that musty smell. Maybe if I could find his cologne in this shithole, I could spray his bed and it would seem like he's here. I don't think Mom is ever going to clean his room. She just keeps the door open and the bedside lamp on like he's going to come home from Joel's tonight."
~Abigail Drummer

Adam's Murder is the transcribed audio diary of Abigail Drummer, Adam's sister. When Adam is brutally murdered, Abby wonders if his addiction and dangerous lifestyle played a part, and when police don't do anything to solve his murder, twenty-year-old Abby must take things into her own hands. She records an audio diary as she discovers just how dark Adam's life was and meets the people closest to him, some of which she didn't know existed. Along the way, she finds herself under the microscope of those she suspects most. Grief, fear, and anger fuel her through this investigation.

This book has also been read on the podcast Indicted Fiction. Each season is a book itself and is narrated by the author herself. You can find the podcast on Alyanna Poe's YouTube channel.

What separates the book from the podcast is the included three-page epilogue that can't be read or listened to *anywhere* but in this book.

Adam's Murder

Alyanna Poe

Dedicated to my grief.

Contents

Hello Reader,

This book was difficult to write. Not because I'm illiterate. Not because I never got a college degree. Not because it's hard to write a book.

I lost my half-brother in 2020. For a year I struggled with mixed feelings of grief and guilt and anger. While writing *Adam's Murder*, I felt this catharsis. I wrote many of these pages through blurred tears; had to stop typing just to wipe the tears away. Many of the things Abigail says to her brother are things I would have liked to have said to my estranged brother. Any chance of that is gone, which is why I think this narrative was so necessary for my growth.

I hope, if you've lost someone, whether you were close or not, that this piece resonates with you and means something to you. *Adam's Murder* helped me grieve, and it's all I can hope for to help someone else through their process.

Yours truly,
Alyanna Poe
2022

PS

It's 2026 when I write this. I've edited this manuscript to improve the reader's experience, and I just wanted to let you know:

It hasn't gotten any easier.

Chapter One: Identification

I promise I didn't murder him!

That's the first thing I told police when they came to tell me my brother was dead.

I meant it as a humorous break in a very tense situation.

The officers did not take it that way.

It was October 18th. The day was warm, so I had left the front windows open while reading Stephen King's Christine. I wasn't too scared by the car, but boy was she brutal. I could only dream of getting over on those that hurt me like that.

That was only three days ago, and life has changed drastically since.

I saw the officers before they got to my door, and my heart sank.

The officer in front had a grey buzzcut, and every line in his face was pulled down into a deep grimace. The fellow behind him appeared to be a younger version of him, with less lines and wrinkles, but just as much sorrow.

It had been three weeks since Adam had gone missing. He was only a year older than me, and having been held back in the third grade, we ended up in the same classes up until we graduated. Despite our lives being forced together, we were never close.

I knew he was dead. I knew before the officer softly rapped his fingers against our apartment door, so gently compared to when they would come to drop off Adam in his drunken stupor.

I placed my bookmark onto the page and closed it, my heart in my stomach as I heard my mother's footsteps coming from the back of the apartment. She turned the corner and asked why I hadn't opened the door.

I told her it was for her. She heard my voice waver and looked at me questioningly as she walked past.

An instinct told me to open it first, to break the tension in the room. I pushed around her, flung open the door, and blurted, *"I promise I didn't murder him!"*

I really don't know why I said it. I think if Adam would've been present, he would have blown a gasket laughing.

The officers looked at me bitterly, the older one glaring harshly. I gave a sheepish smile as he poked his head around me.

"Mrs. Drummer?" he asked. My mother nodded. He spoke softly, yet cold. "Your son, Adam, was found at Star Bend. An investigation has been put into place to find the person that killed him."

My mother fell to her knees, her hands covering her face. I didn't believe it. Before I heard it, I was sure Adam was dead. After I heard it, I was sure he would push past the officers and into the doorway at any second. He'd grin and ask, "What's for dinner?" before plopping onto the couch.

Not minding my mother, the officer said, "We're going to need someone to identify the body."

The idea of seeing Adam dead made me sick, and a thought ran through my mind, something Adam had told me years prior:

"You ever catch me dead, you better burn my body and everything I own."

It had been a very morbid thing to say, especially considering we were at our aunt's funeral, and her husband had been only two seats away when Adam leaned over and whispered.

I suppose identifying the body would be the last time I would get to see him before we dump him somewhere they'll put makeup on him and dress him up. Knowing my parents, they won't let him burn.

With my mother in hysterics, I told the police we would be down shortly, closed the door, and helped her to the couch.

Any minute and Adam would call me. I felt myself checking my phone every few minutes as Mom cried uncontrollably.

I swept away the tears, clawing and pushing them away from my eyes. In no time I was huddled on the couch, curled within my mother's grasp as we sobbed. Half an hour went by before I thought to call my dad. I had no voice left, so in haste I decided to text him.

Adam was found dead.

Looking back on this, I should have called.

Dad didn't respond, rather he busted through the front door not five minutes later and cradled us in his large arms. His face was as broken as ours.

I managed to let him know what the police said, and he dragged us off the couch, gently placing us into our minivan.

The rain had moved in on such a vibrant day. It was more than metaphorical as water sloshed over the windshield wipers.

I clutched my mother's hand from the back seat, the only sounds in the car were our whimpers and the rain mercilessly beating against the roof.

My mind hurt as I thought about never seeing Adam again. A torrent of a sadness I never knew existed flooded my thoughts. It was incomprehensible.

My brother is dead.

I kept repeating it in my mind, but it wasn't real. The statement held no meaning. It held no meaning because it wasn't true.

I felt as if I couldn't walk, falling out of the minivan's door and into the wet parking lot of the coroner's office. Through the lobby and down many fluorescent-lit, white-tiled hallways blurred through tears, we came into a room of metal lockers.

I cried out seeing the white sheet. My mother collapsed before the steel table. My father picked her up, keeping an arm around her.

The coroner looked at us with a glazed stare and gently folded the sheet back, just exposing Adam's pale face. His eyes were wide open and staring at the ceiling. I followed his gaze up to the ceiling to see what he might see if he were capable, temporarily blinding myself with the fluorescent light.

My parents and I huddled around him, my mom touching his face. I gently placed a hand on his cheek, something I had never done when he was alive. It was cold, like lunch meat.

With no trace of harm on his face, and before I could stop the words, I turned to the coroner and asked, "How did he die?"

I've come to regret these four words.

As most stereotypical coroners appear, this man was grim, emotionless, and strikingly free of vitality, bearing resemblance to my deceased brother. Without a word, he whipped back the sheet. Thankfully, it only exposed Adam's upper body, which had been ripped to shreds by what looked like tens, if not hundreds, of bullet wounds. His abdomen looked like hamburger meat, the muscle torn away to expose some of his organs. I swayed on my feet, my eyes glued onto the greyish, foul flesh as my mother hit the ground. With a flick of his wrist, the coroner covered Adam's body.

Just three weeks ago, before Adam had gone missing, he had strutted out into the living room shirtless, pulling a comb through his entire two chest hairs. I had laughed at him then, taking for granted the moment and his genial attitude.

A wave of nausea struck me, crawling from my toes, up through my body, until I threw up my breakfast in a splatter on the white linoleum. I looked up into the coroner's dark eyes. He seemed annoyed, as if the splash on the floor was more of an inconvenience than my dead brother on the table. No sympathy lay in the sharp angles of his face.

The night passed in agony as I lay in bed listening to my mother's cries. At some point I think she either fell asleep or stifled her tears. I looked over at my clock, the green numbers reading one o' eight, and slid out. The tears had dried on my skin, making my face feel rough and raw. My eyes hurt the worst. The space behind them continuously throbbing. I opened my door carefully. Adam's door was open right across from mine, and I made eye contact with him.

Well, a photo of him from last summer's camping trip to Silver Fork. His bedside light was on, the bulb just bright enough to make it appear that he might be in there studying or writing, not that he had done either of those in years. I still wonder if it was my mom or dad that had ventured inside and turned it on.

I quickly crept across the hallway and into his room, the smell of cologne smacking me. I hadn't been in his room since before he'd gone missing. He was lying in bed when I came in. I asked if he had seen my purse.

"What would I know about a purse?" he responded, not looking away from the crack in the ceiling above his bed.

I rolled my eyes, catching sight of the handle under his bed. I bent down and scooped it up, saying, "Well, I guess the cat must have brought it in here."

Adam took my things a lot, but he never stole from me. I always got the things back. Before I'd left the room that night, he grabbed my wrist, sitting up quickly. I looked back, catching a frightened look in his eyes. "Promise me you'll do something good with your life, Abs?"

He never called me Abs. He only called me Babs or Gail Force Winds, a play on my name and the fact that as a child I had flatulence issues. In my hesitation, his grip on my wrist tightened. I nodded, speechless and wondering why every interaction with him *alone* had to be so cryptic. Around my parents and the rest of my family, he was the jester, commonly the butt of every joke, but around me he was dark, sometimes scary. Questions like this one came up often.

He nodded and let go, laying back in the same position. To break the tension, I almost jabbed him in the ribs, but we weren't those kind of siblings, were we?

Adam's room felt empty. The house felt hollow. Pretty soon his bedroom would fill up with that musty smell of an unused place.

I sat on the floor, curling my knees up to my chest. I didn't understand why it had to be him. Isn't the good one supposed to die so the bad one can have a second chance?

Well, Adam wasn't bad, but he didn't live for good either. Who could murder him like that?

I don't care how many classes he skipped. How many gas stations he stole from. Or how many drugs he did. He was Adam, and his existence was for something, right?

He always helped Mrs. Reynolds across the street. He always picked up stray dogs. He would do anything for my parents and me. If there is a God, where is his sympathy?

A piece of paper sat poking out from under Adam's bed, tucked into the bedframe.

Had he hidden it there on purpose? Or had it simply been lost?

I felt wrong as I reached for it. It could have been no more than a doodle or maybe a girl's phone number, but my stomach churned, nonetheless. It was in my fingers before I could pull my hand away, and I flipped it over.

In scrawl I didn't recognize, it said,

"Smith's Hard Stuff."

Chills ran down my spine. That was the last place I knew Adam to be alive.

"I'll be back shortly, my dudes. Going to Smith's for some smokes." I had glanced at him when he said it, happy to have him out of the house and in control of the remote for the first time that day.

My mom told him not to be long and that dinner would be done shortly. By the looks of Adam, food wasn't the first thing on his mind. The lesions had opened up on his jawline again. I watched him dig and scratch at them while we watched TV, scraping at them like a dog scratching an itch.

His demeanor had changed halfway through watching TV. The ads started to irk him, and he bounced his leg up and down, impatiently.

I knew Smith's Hard Stuff well and had seen the man that stood outside that liquor store every night. I could see him through my bedroom window. Most nights I only knew him by the glow of his cigarette. Up until a few years ago, I had really believed that he was Adam's friend. Now that I'm older, I know he's Adam's worst enemy.

Was.

Was his worst enemy.

He was the first person I approached the morning after Adam didn't come home. Never had I spoken a word to this man, only had I heard muffled, short sentences between him and my brother the few times I'd been around.

I walked up to him fast and hot. I was heated for sure, asking—more like yelling— "Where is he?! Where is Adam?"

He looked shocked, his large eyes bugging out further from his slim, scraggily face. He said he didn't know. He said he hadn't seen Adam in two weeks. Two weeks? Adam couldn't go a day without something to boost his mood. How could he have gone two weeks?

The note crinkled in my hand as my fists clenched. It was then that the fog cleared in my mind for the first time since I got the news Adam had gone missing.

He found someone else.

Yesterday, a.k.a. three days after Adam's death, was the day he was to start rehab. It wouldn't be the first time, but maybe this could have been the last time he would need it.

Maybe he could have recovered.

I can't get lost in the *what ifs* right now. Anyway.

I looked at the note again, finally recognizing it as Adam's best friend's handwriting.

Joel.

It was one in the morning, and I really didn't want to get yelled at by Mom for going out so late. A sick thought ran through my mind.

I don't want to end up like Adam either.

I couldn't tell if picking up the note was a good thing or not, but maybe it would lead to something.

Lead to what? Me looking for Adam's murderer?

I went to bed that night with that in my mind. I fell asleep, convincing myself that the police would do their job. That they would bring justice to Adam.

By sunrise I was up and dressed, sitting on the edge of my bed. My poor little thumb nail had been bitten down to a nub as I waited to hear my parents shuffling around. I wasn't the type to leave without a word, especially since Adam's disappearance, and leaving a note would likely give my parents a heart attack, so I had to wait.

In lieu of staring at the ceiling, I pulled out a fresh notebook and decided to start something. I want to write all the things I never could say to Adam, starting with this entry from this morning:

I don't know if I should say hello or if that would be weird. I've never been the religious type, but I think you're still lingering around, and maybe you'll read this someday.

I miss you. I miss waking up and hearing you already arguing with Mom and Dad. It was always about the dumbest shit, and you'd make up so quickly. I miss you coming into my room while I read just to sit beside me. It used to annoy me but now I see you were just trying to be a brother. I even miss the bad and scary stuff. Like sitting in the passenger seat while you drove 110 on the freeway, high out of your mind. I thought we were going to die, but at least it would have been together.

Most of all I miss the idea that someday we might be close. That someday I would be an aunt and you would be an uncle, and we could pretend our childhood meant nothing and be a family.

Now all of that is gone. Now I've got to navigate life alone.

Tears have left some of the ink smudged, but I'll leave this out on my desk, nonetheless. Maybe he'll read it, maybe he won't. I really don't know how dying works.

Having written that, I sat on my bed and stared out the window. People were already bustling around the liquor store despite the sun barely being above the horizon. At the first clink of a coffee cup, I was up and out of my room. I gave them a short version of my plan, well, my lie. I told them I was off to see Joel, to give him a photo I had found of both him and Adam. I told them I hoped it would soften the news. I didn't mention the creepy note. My mother gave me a worried look but let me go.

Out in the hallway, I almost ran into my neighbor. We sheepishly smiled at each other but said nothing. I'm sure she'd heard it all from my mother already.

I'm just realizing that I must have looked terrible. Ratty hair. Puffy, red eyes. Who could blame me though?

Down the stairs I went, the smell of cigarettes spoiling the fresh, morning air. Some of my neighbors would replace their esophagus with an eternally burning cigarette if they could.

Joel lives two blocks away with a roommate I despise, and of course he was the one to open the door.

A little background info on Chuck: he's been obsessed with me since the eighth grade. Adam met Chuck on the kickball field and brought him home, only to have Chuck stand in my bedroom doorway and stare at me while Adam tried to convince him to go outside with him. Ever since then, Chuck has been one step behind me everywhere I go.

Chuck lit up a little at seeing me, but I saw the dark circles under his eyes immediately. I think he noticed me peer around him because he said, "Joel and Adam aren't here."

I scoffed, almost smirking and said, "Well, no that's because Adam is in the morgue."

His face fell like a sack of potatoes off the back of a truck. He asked me to come in, and without anyone I knew there, I declined.

"Adam's dead?" he asked, like I hadn't just said it. "I thought he was missing?" he asked, stepping out his door. I backed away because, well honestly, his presence irks me.

I said, "He was until he wasn't, Chuck. Where can I find Joel?"

He paused, like really paused, so I had to ask again.

"Joel's been gone for three days."

Gone? I asked if he knew where he went, and when he said no, I turned my back and left. Chuck wouldn't know any more than I did, but Joel's mom might.

I stood on her doorstep and wondered why I was there. Joel was a good guy, his mom was even better, always being very hospitable to me and Adam. I hoped for the best and rang the doorbell. In that moment, I decided to give her the photo and break the news.

She opened the door with tears in her eyes. Maria saw the look on my face and hugged me tightly. I hugged her back, thinking I could recognize this woman in any crowd. She stood at least a foot shorter than me, and had beautiful long, dark hair that contrasted against her brown skin. She would always be a beacon of comfort for me.

She invited me inside. I took the invitation, grateful to get out of the cold. When we were sitting comfortably on her warm couch, she said, "Joel's gone missing now, too."

I nodded, taking her hand in mine. My face broke. I had been doing so well hiding the pain. Adam's face, the pale, dead one I had seen the night before, flashed through my mind.

"Oh, Mama, Adam's dead."

Her eyes widened, and she sobbed, clutching at me with weak arms. Together we realized that Joel's fate could very well be the same. We cried in each other's arms much like I had with my parents.

I wondered who could so heinously murder a young man like Adam. Did they know he was afraid of spiders? And that he wouldn't sleep all night if he saw one in the house? Did they know he loved pistachio ice cream and wouldn't order anything if the ice cream shop didn't have that flavor? What about his love of history? Did they know he dressed up as George Washington almost every Halloween until we were thirteen?

Surely, they didn't know all of that as they sprayed him with lead, but I do. I remember it all. No matter how distant we were, no matter his addiction, no matter his confrontational personality, he's still my brother and I still love him.

And I, Abigail Drummer, vow to find my brother's killer.

Chapter Two: Betrayal

Chuck really knows how to push my buttons. It's October 22nd, five days after my brother was found dead, three days after I discovered his best friend has gone missing as well, and one hour after I punched Chuck in the gut.

Not going to lie, it felt wonderful. The wheezing afterwards was just the icing on the cake. I had left Mama Maria's, teary eyed and woeful, to return home, where I isolated for two days. Alone in my room, I wrote another letter to Adam and cried until I finally felt like I couldn't cry anymore. The dreaded insomnia has taken its place in my life again, causing my mind to race while everyone around me sleeps. In those races, I realized I'm no closer to an answer about Adam's killer. The police haven't made contact since we IDed Adam on the 18th.

This morning I came out of my room to find my parents huddled on the couch in silence. They stared forward at the dark TV screen, unbeknownst to me. I made coffee, knowing I would need it, and that's when my mom finally turned on the TV.

We watched the local news, catching the tail end of an interview with a local artist, the weather, and this morning's traffic. A reporter came on screen after a commercial break. She stood at an intersection only three blocks away from our apartment building, smiling. Opening her big, red lips, she said,

"Tod, I'm happy to report that crime in Olivehurst has dropped a staggering sixty percent in the last five years!"

I grimaced, knowing this to be a lie. Before she could open her mouth again, my father snatched up the remote and shut the TV off.

We sat in silence as I drank my coffee, and I decided today would be the day I do some real investigating. Getting dressed, I caught sight of Chuck at Smith's Hard Stuff. You can't miss Chuck's red hair. Not to mention he's like two feet taller than everyone. As I pulled on my pants, I noticed he approached the man Adam called *Slim*. Again, Slim told me he knew nothing, which he probably didn't if Adam had found another source, but Chuck wasn't aware of that.

By his body language, I could tell he was mad. I watched as things quickly heated up. Chuck started waving his arms around and Slim shoved him back. That's when I got moving.

I raced to get my shit together and out the door. Running down the stairs felt eternally long, like those summer evenings when I knew I only had a small amount of time left to play but had to get down the stairs before I could get on my bike. I turned the corner and ran across the street, calling for Chuck. He whipped around, his eyes blazing, but before I could get to him, he turned around again, this time punching Slim in the side of the head.

I don't know why I felt the urge to protect Slim or Chuck, but I knew the only way to do that was to end the fight. I grappled Chuck from behind, ducking under his flailing arms before getting him to turn around. When he tried to shove me aside, I raised my fist into his gut, using all my upward momentum. He doubled over, wheezing as Slim scuttled around the corner. I grabbed his arm and dragged him away from the store as he gasped.

"What's your problem?" I asked.

He started crying. *Jesus Christ*, this town has cried enough tears to float the ark.

We sat on the steps of my apartment building, and when Chuck put his arm around me, I didn't stop him. I didn't have any more tears to cry, but I could understand his pain. His two closest friends were gone, and I'm sure he'd come to the conclusion that Joel most likely suffered the same fate as Adam.

We sat there for a while, staring at the street until I got a text from my mom. When I stood up and said, "Hey, I gotta go up to my apartment, see ya later," Chuck's eyes welled with tears again.

"I'll stop by sometime soon," I said, regretfully, as I walked up the steps. I heard him snivel before he got up and left.

Mom's text said, "I need your help." I managed to keep my cool in front of Chuck, but I dreaded going inside, fearing more tears or bad news.

She asked me to open a pickle jar. I couldn't have been more amused and annoyed, but most of all, I was just glad she wasn't lying on the couch with a pillow smooshed into her face anymore. She wrapped the pickle into a tortilla with cheese and lunch meat, asking if I wanted one. Bile ran up my throat. I was thankful for the nearby garbage can as I heaved up coffee. My throat got the worst of it.

She must've said, "All you had to say was *no*."

Well, now I'm in my room, wrapped up in about five blankets. It's freezing in here, but Mom insists it's warm enough. I think I saw my breath earlier.

Since I've been sitting here, I haven't seen Slim at his post. Chuck must have scared the wits out of him.

I've never done drugs, and booze makes me sick, so I could never understand Adam's addiction. I knew he needed it. I knew when he needed it. But I could never understand why.

Was life with us so bad? Could he really not live without it? It all started when I was fifteen, four long years ago. He was sixteen, but we were in the same classes, had been since the third grade. He just started acting different. Started arguing with Mom and Dad about trivial things. His acne blossomed, growing worse and worse as he dug at it. Looking at his face while his body lay on that cold, steel table, I saw for the first time just how deep those craters he'd made were, his cheeks and forehead were pocked with them.

He started stealing things, and not just from gas stations. School electronics were going missing. A random tire, like a full-sized car tire, would end up in his bedroom. But he never stole from me or my parents. I think he knew better, or his conscience was just strong enough to protect us.

Once he even showed up with a random car. I suppose I can say this now that he's gone. I don't think the police have any jurisdiction over dead people.

So, he showed up with this car while I was out riding my bike home from school. He almost clipped me with it as I turned on our street and as I go to throw my water bottle, I noticed it was Adam. He parked upfront, got out, and leaned against it like it was a classic. The paint was peeling from the hood, and I could see the torn headliner hanging down over the backseat, but he was *proud*.

"Where'd you get that?" I asked.

"Mind yer beeswax, Gail."

I *hated* when he did his cowboy voice.

That car didn't last long. Mom saw it and flipped her lid. A day later, the charred remains of it were found at a beach not too far from where Adam's body was discovered. That's when I knew it was stol–

[click]

I'm back. That was…Joel. He just showed up here. I'm happy to report that he's not dead, but he's also not the same. He insisted on taking me to Geraldo's, a little Mexican joint down the road. We sat at one of the picnic tables under the restaurant's awning after he parked in the gravel lot beside the small shack. The drive over was quiet, which is odd for Joel. He's generally very talkative, especially when he's using, which would be about as long as Adam was. The interior of his car was disgusting as usual, filled to the brim with fast food garbage and the smell of BO. Despite this, I noticed the acne along his jawline is clearing up, and I've got to wonder if maybe he's trying to get clean. While waiting for the food, I thought it best to finally ask where he had disappeared to, and if he knew about Adam.

In a mess of words, he didn't entirely explain where he had been but rather ended with a question.

"Life here isn't going anywhere, is it?"

My eyes dropped to his shoes, which were off to the side of the bench he was sitting on. The white undersides were heavily stained green, like he had been trudging through grass for days. "Have you seen Mama?" I asked, looking into his dark eyes. The bags under them seemed heavier than usual.

He shook his head, twisting his lips to the side. "I haven't seen her in about a week."

"Adam's dead." The words slipped from my lips as they called his name at the counter. His hand was on mine in an instant, yet his face didn't change.

"I'm so sorry, Abby."

I expected more tears, but Joel simply stood up and retrieved our food. A chasm inside me opened a little further. Had I wanted to cry in this public space with one of my closest friends? Not really, but I did want him to show something that at least resembled the Joel I knew.

I say closest friend because I have no friends outside of the people my family members know. My mother's hairdresser and I play cards on the weekend. I meet Mama Maria at the grocery store sometimes so we can get coffee and a pastry. My dad's coworker, Julianne, comes over sometimes and we clip coupons together like two old ladies. Everyone I knew in school left my life when I graduated. I've been thinking about college, but I don't think I'm eligible for any scholarships, and I don't even have a car.

Joel has been there for every birthday since I was twelve. I've spent countless nights bundled up next to him and my brother watching horror movies. We may not know a lot about each other, but he's just been a part of my life so long that it doesn't really matter. He's family.

Adam is my family. I'm the only one who knew his darker side, but, but maybe that means we were extra close. I've always felt so distant from him, but maybe those cold, awkward moments were something meaningful, a side Adam couldn't show to others.

Joel is acting weird. And I need to know why.

He sat down, handing me my foil wrapped burrito, the one that now sits heavy in my gut. I had lost my appetite breaking the news to him but didn't want to seem off. Can't have him suspicious of me, right?

He ate his nachos like he hadn't seen food in a year, then stared at me as I nibbled on my burrito. It was awkward to say the least, but then he spoke up.

"Adam and I were fighting the night he disappeared."

Chills blossomed on my arms and legs. Would he really admit guilt right here at Geraldo's? Around all these people? Was Joel capable of murdering his best friend?

I think he read the thoughts I was having like my face was a billboard because he explained himself quickly.

Turns out Adam was getting his fix from a new source, something Slim had already told me. His product wasn't doing the job, and Adam wasn't having it, so he started going down a few streets to a man named Ricardo.

Joel's words were, "I told him not to go see him. I told him he was bad business, but he told me to fuck off and left."

I asked if that was it, and he said that was the last time he had seen Adam.

I didn't believe him. Still don't. I knew that Adam had found a new source, but I don't think that was the last time Joel saw him.

Just as I was finishing up my burrito, a car drove by and honked. Joel smiled and waved as they continued down the street. I didn't recognize the car, so I asked who it was. He snapped me a dirty look.

"Don't you ever mind your business, Abby?"

I was taken aback. Instead of sticking around for Joel's mood swings, I got up, threw away the rest of the burrito, and walked toward my place, which was only about two miles back.

He didn't follow, and I was glad, that is, until he caught me at the stairs to my apartment. In my head too deep, I was thinking how much of Adam's life was hidden from my parents and I, and how much Joel knew about my brother that I wasn't even aware of, when Joel's hand clamped down on my arm. I yanked it away, clutching the stair's railing tight and making the first step. He asked me to come to his place, so he could talk to me in private. I told him no, but he grabbed my waist and hoisted me away from the stairs. He set me down before I made the decision between punching him or letting him take me. I decided on the latter. Clasping his fingers through mine, he led me to his car. I wondered if Chuck would be at their place, somewhat hoping he would be. I'd never been fully alone with Joel before.

He drove like he stole the car, taking off before I even had my seatbelt on, and when he slammed the brakes, a pistol slid out between my feet. It wasn't my first time seeing a gun, obviously, but it was still shocking to say the least. I had seen Joel with an arsenal of weapons, but he couldn't hide them better than that? I lightly pushed it back into place with the heel of my sneaker, and before I knew it, we were at his place.

Chuck wasn't there, and I thought better than to inquire about him. Joel knows I despise Chuck. Always have... always will, and asking about him would only raise a cherry red flag.

I don't understand how people live in such filth. Is it a guy thing? Is that it? And he didn't even try to conceal his addiction. No embarrassment at all. I knew the bong on the table was Chuck's. He's always been a stoner, but the bags and bags of pills everywhere had to be Joel's. The glass coffee table, the one with condensation rings on it that has always driven me mad, had a few streaks of powder on it.

I just don't understand the need, and I hope I never will.

Joel had that look in his eyes as he sat on the couch, like he was lost, tired, and dazed. I sat in the recliner across from him and averted my eyes as he snorted a line. It was a loud, obnoxious sound that I loathed.

He sighed and said, "Why are you so pretty?"

My heart thudded in my chest. No one had called me pretty since the incident with Vinny. Freshman year I had come over to Mama Maria's looking for Adam. He'd skipped out on school that day, and I was coming over to tell him he owed me for covering his ass again. The new kid was over with Adam and Joel, playing some nasty video game. Vinny from the East Coast. He asked who the hot chick was when I walked into the room, and that's when Adam gave him a beating that inevitably sent him back to the East Coast. It was no skin off my back. I didn't like the barbarians my brother kept in company. Ever since then, no one has complimented me in front of Adam.

Now I guess Adam isn't here to protect me.

I laughed it off and asked if he was going to tell me why he brought me over. He told me to slow down, to take a second to breathe. The convo went swimmingly.

"You ever just relax, Abby?"

I shook my head.

"You ever just sit there and let your mind go blank?"

I shook my head again, looking around the room, rather than into his wild eyes. I had never seen so many pills in one place before. I don't know how he's going to snort all of those. Maybe he's having a party?

Anyway, he said, "You ever been high?"

I rolled my eyes. "No, Joel. I'm trying to get out of this hellhole." I didn't want to admit that I'm terrified of any substance. I won't even take the pills my doctor prescribed me for my eczema. I think the years of watching Adam struggle with his lows broke any curiosity I might've had.

He seemed mad, like I insulted him.

Adam was a very dark person when we were alone, but he wanted me to do good. Years prior I had walked in on him pulling out his pipe. He kept it "hidden" in a compartment he'd cut into his backpack. It amazed me the things he would do to keep his addiction a secret, yet the entire town knew him as a drug addicted adolescent. He ran up on me, shut the door, and grabbed my shoulders. I looked deep into his dark eyes, and he had that lost, longing look.

That was back before his cheeks had sunk into his face. Before the violent picking had given him craters. Before all the color had drained from his skin.

Pipe in hand, he pulled me close, our noses touching, and said, "Don't ever do this shit. No matter who offers you it. No matter what it is. Don't do it."

There Joel sat across from me, twiddling a pill between his fingers.

I'm sketching what it looked like right now, just so that maybe I can start keeping track of what's going on.

Joel looked at me and said, "Abby, I think you'd like this. It's like the best sugar high times a hundred."

I sat there, dumbfounded. It was as if he were trying to convince a child to take it.

"Is this what Adam was taking?"

He hesitated, looking down at the pill. "Just try it, Abby."

I got up. "I don't have time for this shit," I said, almost running for the door.

"No matter who offers you it. No matter what it is."

Adam was always there to protect me.

I heard Joel get up as I undid the secondary bolt lock. I didn't even realize he had locked up the place when we got there. His footsteps came after me fast, and as I reached for the deadbolt, the lock swiveled, and the door opened inward.

I fell into Joel just as Chuck pushed his way into the house.

"Oh, hey guys." He said it so *stupidly*, with a gleeful innocence to the situation.

Joel was taken aback, gasping from behind me as I slithered out the door. Chuck called after me, but I ran through the parking lot, only slowing to catch my breath when I was a block from home.

I need a car.

I need…I need a gun.

Adam was there *every time* I was out with his friends. Adam was there every time I went to the grocery store. Every time I went clothes shopping. Every time I needed him.

And now he's gone.

I have to protect myself now.

[click]

His room is starting to get that musty smell. Maybe if I could find his cologne in this shithole, I could spray his bed and it would seem like he's here. I don't think Mom is ever going to clean his room. She just keeps the door open and the bedside lamp on like he's going to come home from Joel's tonight.

She stepped out to see the neighbor, and Dad is asleep on the couch. I think I have enough time.

It's not in his backpack, under his bed, or in his underwear drawer. I regret that last one.

I'll try the closet, but I haven't got a lot of time.

[rustling]

Shit. He still has a card I gave him in third grade. It was just propped up in his closet. It's a heart, and it says... "We're brother and sister."

That really describes us, I guess. I can't imagine why he would keep something like that.

[thud]

Oh, yes. Yes. Adam had one treasured pistol, and it's in my hands now.

Do you think he'd want me to have it?

[clinking]

Oh, there's some ammo in the shoe box it was in. Nice.

What—what's that?

Shit, Mom's back.

[click]

Okay, I got it back to my room unsuspected. I remember the first time I shot this baby, but there was a note in the box. I almost threw it aside, but I saw my name on it. It says,

"To Abigail,"

I don't like this.

"I'm going to die before you, my honor roll, teacher's pet, book-loving bitch of a sister. In case I don't give this to you before I die, this note here is proof that I, Adam R. Drummer, am gifting you this gun. It is yours to keep, cherish, and shoot people with."

I...it's Adam's handwriting. There's something on the back in really bad scrawl.

[paper rustling]

"Don't trust Joel."

[click]

What do I even say? I have no words. Mom caught me crying in my bed. Luckily, I hid the box before melting down.

After I cried on her shoulder for a solid thirty minutes, she gave me the news.

Adam's funeral is tomorrow.

Chapter Three: The Funeral

I brought the cat to the funeral. Mr. Chubbz is as much a part of the family as I am, so I felt like he needed to be there. He remained in his carrier most of the time, staring up at me from the chair next to mine. He was on his best behavior, and I think bringing him out of the house helped him out of his depression. Out of all of us, I'm pretty sure Adam was Mr. Chubbz' favorite.

Today was rough, and I'm just glad to be in bed, but I met someone important, so here's how the day went:

We woke up early and dressed for the funeral. I don't really have any formal attire, so I wore black jeans and a black long sleeve. I think Adam would have approved. I felt guilty taking time to attend his funeral, like I should have been further investigating his murder. As I was brushing my hair, I realized paying my respects to him and being there for my family was equally as important.

The police hadn't been in contact with us, and I didn't expect their presence at the funeral. This morning I really did believe it was entirely in my hands to find who killed Adam.

We got there early and helped set things up, and when Adam was carried in, I felt sick. It was like setting up a birthday party with the birthday kid right there, just standing and staring in agonizing silence. Okay, it wasn't like that but that's the only way I can put it that feels right.

By 10 a.m., the church was very crowded. Like, there was barely enough room to get around, and only when someone realized I was the deceased's sister, did a couple stand up and give me their seats in the front. I didn't recognize half of the people and wondered how many Adam truly knew.

Some I recognized from the NA meetings I had attended with him. He had never *asked* me to come with, but before meetings he would come in my room, sit on the edge of my bed, and sigh. I heard from a friend of Adam's that dealers would go to meetings and try to get clients, so I always felt big and bad going with him, like I was his personal bodyguard.

A few of them looked better, clean, while others looked the same, if not worse.

It was an open casket funeral since the part of Adam that was destroyed could be shoved into a suit. As I stood over him, touching the casket, I couldn't help but feel a pang of guilt. He didn't want to be buried like this. He wanted to be cremated.

I was nervous as the pastor read a generic eulogy. I knew after him my dad would speak. Then my mom. Then me. I had written up something meaningful, flowery even, but when I got up in front of everyone, when all those eyes hit me, that speech in my hands no longer felt relevant.

To my best recollection, this is what I said,

"Clearly Adam was loved by many. I see many faces I don't even recognize, and I lived with Adam."

My voice cracked when I said Adam, and I watched everyone's eyes widen. My mother had already put everyone through a speech forced between sobs, and my dad's speech was monotone, dark, and very vague. He only referred to Adam as "my son," seeming to refuse to say Adam's name.

I continued on, stifling my tears with a forced smile.

"Despite Adam's struggles, he always remained a beam of light in the lives of everyone he met. He was candid and fun and always so true to himself."

Here I paused. Thoughts raced through my mind, and for a moment I thought I would collapse in a fit of tears. Then I made eye contact with my mom. She looked up at me, eyes wet and mouth drawn down into a deep frown. I was all they had left. So suddenly forced into being an only child. I took a deep breath.

"Adam knew his lifestyle was going to lead to something bad. He told me himself. And as many of you know, he tried to better himself. I don't know why he was taken from us, and I don't know if it had anything to do with his struggles, but he was on the road to recovery."

I realized I was rambling about Adam's addiction, so I moved on.

"He had big plans, and they all involved the community. For years he looked for the perfect place to put a skatepark. And next month he was scheduled to speak in front of townhall to propose it."

Here I felt the tears roll down my cheeks. I had to keep it together.

"He—"

Joel walked into the church, and a burning started in the pit of my stomach. I was enraged he didn't show up but showing up late was so much worse.

"Don't trust Joel."

What did the note mean? Besides the obvious to not trust Joel, I had no context or reasoning to not trust Joel.

Everyone was staring at me.

"He tried to be a force in the community. He wanted change and betterment for Olivehurst. Trust me, I would get stuck listening to him ramble on about how bad the roads are here and the way homeless people are treated." I laughed, thinking of all the times he would hit a pothole and scream about it. It seemed to lighten the crowd as I'm sure they thought the same things. The tears were heavy now, dripping down my chin and onto my fake, flowery speech. "And he was right." I took a deep, shaky breath as the pastor stood to take my place. "He was right."

He put a hand on my shoulder and guided me down the steps. I guess that was my time.

When I sat down, no one was there to comfort me besides Mr. Chubbz, and he wouldn't turn around in his carrier to face me. So, there I sat with Mr. Chubbz's butt facing me as I listened to the drone of the pastor. Everyone bent their heads down in prayer. I craned my neck up to look at the ceiling. The rafters were only stained, nothing fancy. Everyone's whispers took me out of my thoughts. All these people whispering, hoping my brother's soul made it to heaven, knowing damn well in their religion, he was a sinner.

I wish it would have been me.

The church would be empty save for my parents and Adam. The pastor hated me and probably wouldn't attend. I had egged this church too many times. Mr. Chubbz would be back home, curled up on Adam's bed, surely waiting for him to come home.

Why wasn't it me?

I'm awkward and antisocial. Adam knew everyone in town.

I looked around myself, so taken aback by all the people present. All the people that cared.

Was I jealous?

Yeah. I was.

Aunt Marie caught me looking around and gave me a nasty glare over her folded hands. As everyone finished up their prayers with *Amen*, I stared at the white casket at the front of the room. I saw myself laying in it, folded hands and makeup so carefully done. I saw Adam crying over my body, my parents two stony figures in the background, the rest of the church *empty*.

I wish I had gotten to know him better. Would he even cry at my funeral? Surely, he would. I was with him all the time… but was I really *with* him?

He confided nothing to me. He dragged me along with him, yet I was never really included. Just a side character off in the background of his life. He was Adam. I was Abigail. Together "we're brother and sister" as that card in his closet said.

I didn't miss him the times he was out of the house. I didn't crave his "affection." I only dealt with it and came along when I felt like he would get mad if I refused.

Damn bastard had to leave. He had to leave me behind with all these fucked up feelings.

And now the cat's gone, too.

My parents and I said one final goodbye before we moved outside to the cemetery. My parents insisted on him being buried in the church's graveyard despite Adam being about as Christian as a Buddhist.

It was so hard to see the closed casket. I stood there, cat carrier in hand, when I thought about never seeing Adam's face again, not in person at least. Looking around, everyone had someone to cry with. My parents held each other, sobbing softly. My aunts held their husbands, and my cousins held their siblings. So, I unzipped the cat carrier as they lowered my brother into the ground. I wanted to hold something, even if it was our rancid black cat that hated me from the day we got him. My hand reached in, but Mr. Chubbz dodged it.. I snatched him out and tried to hold him to my chest when he squealed and lashed out. His claw got me right under the eye, which stung like a bitch. I held onto him tightly, but he squirmed from my grasp, falling into my brother's grave.

Adam's coffin was a foot before the surface of his grave by the time Mr. Chubbz fell in. Somehow, he slipped through the lowering mechanism, sliding into that foot tall cavity between the dirt and Adam's coffin. I yelled, all eyes on me, but the device was stuck. The cemetery worker tried to reel back the lever, to get the coffin to stop, but it was too late.

Mr. Chubbz mewled as the coffin crushed him, and there I stood, dumbfounded, as the entertainment for the funeral.

My father was the first to yell, questioning why I had brought the cat out in the first place. I saw his sisters snicker, and I know I heard,

"Well, someone's got to be the family fuck up now."

I hate this place. I hate this family. I hate this world. Those closest to you always know where to stab you, and I'm sick of it. I'm sick of it all.

[click]

I apologize. I put my brother in the ground today, and this audio diary isn't for me to spew my feelings into. It's to keep track of what I know about Adam's death. And I learned something new today.

The drive to the banquet hall was quiet, save for a few sniffles here and there. Mr. Chubbz's empty carrier stared at me the whole ride. And when we arrived at the hall, I saw it was mainly family. Most of the people from NA had left, much to my discontent. Now I only had the beady eyes of my extended family to look forward to.

The food was terrible. I picked at it sitting alone at a table in the corner of the hall. If Adam had been there, I think he would have silently taken my hand and snuck me out to pizza or something that didn't taste like lukewarm food from the garbage disposal.

When I looked up to see kids playing pin the tail on the donkey under the close watch of my Aunt Betty, I almost lost it. Yes, I've heard of "celebration of life," but pin the tail on the donkey? After a funeral? Shit, during the wake? God, Adam's wake was at a banquet hall next to an old folks' home.

Anyway, I felt sick. I felt sick that there were kids laughing during Adam's wake. I felt sick that the rest of my family hates me. And I felt sick that I killed Adam's cat with his coffin.

But most of all I felt sick that we had laid Adam in the ground. I wanted to run back to the cemetery, dig him up, even if it was with my bare hands, and throw open the coffin lid. I would hold him, hug him like I never did when he was alive.

I imagined he would be cold. He'd be heavy and limp, and it would take everything in me to pick him up into a sitting position so that I could look into his dead, dark eyes. So that I could see just how empty his body was. He would stink of embalming fluid and blood. I could smell it all above the casket. Maybe his shirt would lift up in my throws of sorrow and a chewed-up intestine would plop out.

I scooped up a spoonful of peas, and when I drew them near my mouth, they smelled not of peas, but of embalming fluid and blood.

I rushed to the bathroom, under the gazes and glares of my family members, and hurled the food into the nearest toilet. Quite frankly, it tasted better coming back up.

When I got out of the stall to wash my face, I realized I was in the men's bathroom. A man, probably in his forties, light brown hair, came out of the stall next to the one I had rushed into, concern plastered onto his face.

I quickly apologized and tried to leave, but he told me not to worry and asked me to stay. I turned around, expecting him to approach me or something strange. He was calmly washing his hands when he introduced himself as Dr. Bleu, Adam's counselor.

We left the rank bathroom and sat at the table where my cold peas and brisket sat. He asked how I was doing, and I couldn't answer honestly. I couldn't tell this stranger that I wanted to exhume my brother an hour after burying him just so I could prop him up in his room like he would wake up one day. The silence gave him the answer he needed as he continued to talk about Adam.

I knew Adam was seeing many doctors, but I had never met any of them. This man seemed nice enough, considering he got paid to be nice to people. I wanted to ask things about Adam but wasn't sure if I was allowed to. Without any prompting from me, Dr. Bleu suddenly opened up about Adam.

He was going through a severe depressive episode before he went missing and had asked for an emergency appointment with Dr. Bleu the week before he was announced missing. In that appointment, Adam dumped things on him even Dr. Bleu didn't know about.

For one, Adam didn't want to get clean. He had found a better drug, something that made him feel more alive than any other drug he had been on. He said he felt focused and reliable on this pill. Here I asked what the pill looked like. Sadly, Dr. Bleu wasn't sure, but he did look at me funny when I asked.

Adam was dead set on getting a job, something I had known for a while, but Dr. Bleu enlightened me that Adam had gone through over forty job interviews from July to October. After a look at his record, many businesses declined him.

I couldn't blame them. On the outside, Adam looked like a rough, mean guy with an even rougher, meaner addiction. And his records included words like "assault with a deadly weapon" and "arson."

The most interesting thing Dr. Bleu had to tell me was, Adam was seeing a girl.

Adam? With a girl?

I had never even seen Adam look at a girl, let alone ask one out, and we were in the same classes since third grade. He never had a girl over and never spoke of anyone catching his eye.

But there were the words, right out of Dr. Bleu's mouth.

"He often spoke of a girl named Chantelle. He had been seeing her since January."

Almost a whole year with this girl!

But Dr. Bleu had some bad news. Chantelle seemed to be a bad influence. I felt a flash of hot anger when he told me this, and I asked if he knew more about her, not letting on that I was going to hang on to every bit of information about her so I could find her myself. He said Adam was very vague about her, always avoiding her physical appearance and last name, despite how many times Dr. Bleu had tried to pry it out of him.

"I think he was afraid I would find out who she was," he said.

A girl. Adam with a girl. A girl that was a bad influence. Tomorrow, I will find her. Adam's phone was on his nightstand last I checked, and all his passcodes have been the same since we were kids. 4200. Our apartment building's address.

So, with nothing else to talk about, Dr. Bleu left, and when I looked up to the rest of the room, it was empty. Even my parent's table was empty. I rushed outside just behind Dr. Bleu and saw my parents sitting on a bench in the sun. My dad had his arm around Mom, and her blonde hair glittered in the sun next to my dad's grey spikes. He'd been gelling his hair like that for as long as I could remember.

It was a moment I didn't want to interrupt. They looked calm, not happy, but calm. No frowns, no tears. Just *existence*.

My dad saw me and waved me over. They said they were going to take me out to dinner since the food was so terrible. My empty stomach was pleased but as I got into the back seat of our van, I was sad.

The family left without a word to me. I realize I was talking to someone, but… a simple wave or a short goodbye would have sufficed.

"Do you think the rest of the family cares about Adam?" I blurted, breaking a tense silence as we drove across town.

This elicited a sharp glare from my mother. She sighed and said, "I don't know., but I wonder the same."

At least I wasn't alone in my thoughts.

Luigi's neon sign lit up the woeful afternoon I was having, and my stomach growled. Last time we had been there, Adam ordered three virgin martinis and got us kicked out by yelling DEEZ NUTS repeatedly. My parents had been laughing as they kicked us out, but I was sorely upset that I couldn't finish their *divine* fettuccine Alfredo I had ordered. Ah, my lactose intolerant gut was in for a *treat*.

We sat in a big booth in the corner of the restaurant where I could see the place in its time capsule-esque beauty. The burgundy carpet omitted cigarette smoke dating back to the nineteen-eighties, and the stained-glass windows embodied everything I thought a church from the seventies would look like. It was one of my favorite places. Luigi's has all the good food. Pizza. Pasta. Salad with the unhealthiest dressings and toppings. Calzones. *Garlic bread.*

I just wish we would have been there for better reasons.

The waitress took our order, and I got up to use the restroom. My parents must have thought this was their only chance.

As I sat in the booth, drying my hands on my pants, I noticed a grin on both of their faces, something I hadn't seen in almost a month. I eyed them before the clapping started.

"Happy, happy birthday", the staff called as they carried over a lava cake with a single pink and white candle.

Oh, right. It's my birthday today. I'm officially twenty-years-old.

Yay.

How this event had slipped past my mind, I'm not sure. I'm just sure that me crying in front of the staff was not the highlight of their day. Adam loved lava cakes. Like *loved* them, even more than pistachio ice cream, and there I was eating one the day we put him in the ground.

One could consider it a celebration of his life, but it made me sick that he wasn't there to split it with me.

What made it worse was, as the staff was doing their little song and dance, I was eyeing each of their name tags like a detective. I hoped to just see a Chantelle or a Shantel or a Chantal. All that was there were two Emmas and a Mary. This search is going to take a while if I don't have the resources I think I do.

As I was slowly putting away that lava cake in hopes that my fettuccine alfredo would come out soon, lo and behold, Chuck walked into the establishment. I tried to duck further into the booth, but we had already made eye contact.

My parents glanced at me and asked what was wrong. I said some weirdo came into the restaurant, and that's when Chuck met us at our table. I'd seen him at the funeral, but he had seemed so deep in his thoughts, so deep in his grief. I wondered what he was doing here when my parents insisted he eat with us. With a sigh, I scooted over, letting him slip in next to me. He quickly explained why he chose Luigi's, ensuring my parents that the banquet food was great.

"This was Adam's favorite. I thought coming here would help honor his memory."

The statement brought a fresh onslaught of tears that I forced back behind a bite of lava cake.

His favorite? We shared a favorite? All my life Adam seemed to purposely hate the things I loved, as I imagine most brothers do, but there was Chuck telling me this was Adam's favorite place.

Maybe Chuck knows more about Adam than I could ever imagine. Maybe I should keep him around.

I don't know.

Dinner was alright. Chuck ate his food between stories about Adam, and, in all honesty, it was the nicest I had felt in a long time. I felt crossed between crushed and giggly as we regaled in stories about Adam's quick wit and nasty sense of humor. I would laugh, only to be struck with the fact that he's not with us anymore.

Adam may be gone, but he won't be forgotten.

[sigh]

And I'm off to bed. I need to be up early tomorrow so I can search for *Chantelle*. I couldn't bring myself to ask Chuck about her in front of my parents, but if Adam's phone brings me no luck, I may have to venture over to Chuck's if Joel isn't there.

I just hope everything I'm doing has a purpose. If not only to grieve, I hope to really find who killed him and bring that murderer to justice. Lord knows I won't stop until I do.

Chapter Four: Discovery

She lives in the same fucking apartment complex as us.

Apartment 73A.

Woke up bright and early just to fiddle with Adam's phone. Turns out his password was a little more complicated than I expected. Instead of it being our building number like I thought, it was in fact the date we got Mr. Chubbz, which was only a few days after Adam's twelfth birthday. May they both rest in peace.

I quickly found Chantelle, considering she's the only girl in Adam's phone, and scrolled through their text messages. They were seeing each other for sure, but by Dr. Bleu's description, I thought Adam was getting ready to propose. She seemed mildly interested, giving one- or two-word responses while Adam asked a lot of questions, some pretty embarrassing.

Here's something that made me laugh until I realized how sad it really was:

"What's your favorite flower?" Adam asked at 8:54 p.m.

"Don't have one," Chantelle responded at 12:13 a.m.

"Well, what am I supposed to bring you?" Adam asked at 12:14 a.m.

"Something fun," she said at 12:56 a.m. followed by a winky face and a pill emoji.

I laughed at Adam's willingness to bring her flowers until I saw just how cruel this girl was. She really wasn't a good influence after all.

I couldn't find her address and, after accidentally reading some pretty *personal* texts, I decided to search their chat instead. Typing in *Address* got me nothing. *House* was just as useless *Place* didn't help either. After ten more tries, I was worn down to looking up synonyms for *home* and *address*.

No use. None of them brought anything up. I wondered where this girl lived, sitting on my bed and looking out at Smith's Hard Stuff. Out of the selfies I had seen her send Adam, I didn't recognize this girl, then again, she wasn't anything special. I guess it made sense that Adam would be into a shallow girl. He never really thought about his own wellbeing all that often.

I wondered if she had ever been in our apartment, and that's when I searched *apartment*.

I'm in apartment 73A.

Followed by a duck faced selfie. I was just glad it wasn't another tit pic.

73A was all the way across the apartment complex in the newer buildings.

I could be there in five minutes.

Well, that's if I rode my bike really fast, but I chose to walk. I grabbed one of Adam's chains, one of the ones with green stains in the creases, and stuffed it in my pocket. A little gift from the grave might soften her up enough to talk, or so I thought. Adam's gun sat heavy in the pocket of my cargo pants. I was wearing the ones my mother calls, "boyish," but they concealed the weapon well. Seven bullets in the mag, and a secondary mag in my back pocket, just like Adam used to carry.

As I approached the door, I noticed the doormat that said *Blessed* and the fuchsia-colored curtains in the windows. It was bound to be a fun day. She answered the door in a nightgown short enough to see just the crest of her butt cheeks. I think it was something my mom calls *lingerie*.

"I don't want any girl scout cookies," she said, trying to close the door.

I told her I wasn't here for that, and she told me she wasn't interested in my religion. So, I flashed Adam's chain and said,

"I've got bad news."

Her mouth dropped open when she saw the chain, and she quickly asked where I got it.

Despite my instincts, I asked if I could come inside. Hesitating, she let me in.

Those fuchsia curtains were only the beginning. I couldn't keep my eyes in one place for too long, from the tiger striped couch to the clearly faux polar bear rug, this place came straight from an eighty's porno, or so I've heard. She told me to sit down, and just in time to complete the porno, a man walked in from the back room, wearing only a leopard print thong. I got the sense she enjoyed animal print, even her nightgown had a peacock feather print on it. She rushed him back into the room and closed the door, telling him she had some business to discuss.

Again, she asked where I got the chain as I handed it to her.

"It was on Adam's nightstand."

Her eyes narrowed on me, and she snapped, "As it should be. Who are you to take it from him?"

I asked her how she knew of the chain. She said she gave it to him as a gift and asked in return why it was any of my business.

"I'm Adam's sister, Abigail."

Her gaze did not soften.

"And, in case you didn't know, Adam's dead."

She covered her mouth with her hand and closed her eyes. Calmly, she said, "I had no idea."

"We had his funeral yesterday." At this point, I really felt no remorse for her.

She cried. I had no tears to shed with this woman, but I told her that I spoke to one of Adam's close friends, not wanting to relay to her that Adam had a counselor, and he said that Adam was very fond of her. She smiled lightly, and that's when the man came out of the room fully dressed. He slipped her something, and I watched her count what it was.

Before I could stop myself, I asked, "Was Adam a customer?"

She looked at me with wide eyes, shaking her head. "No." Tears ran down her cheeks in rivers as she caught her breath. The man left without a word, closing the door quietly behind him. "No, Adam was my everything."

I sat there quietly as she told me what she could. Here's what I can recollect:

She had met Adam through Slim. Slim is Chantelle's uncle, and for a while he lived with her in her apartment. One day Slim brought Adam back to her place for a beer, but she thinks Slim was trying to set them up. It worked.

"Adam was my knight," her words, not mine. "He was going to get clean. I was going to get clean. He was going to get a job, and I was going to be right there. I helped him with his resumes. I applied to some of the same jobs, but we never got picked." She looked down at the wad of cash in her hand and threw it on the carpet forcefully. "I hate this life." She was crying hard now. "Adam was more than just a party friend or a fuck buddy. We were in it together. We wanted out." She picked up a wristband from the side table beside the recliner she was sitting on and handed it to me. It said, "One Day Sober. One Day Closer to Redemption."

She continued on. "I attended rehab like we were supposed to. I was so mad when he didn't show up. When he didn't answer my calls, I thought he had ghosted me." She asked when, how, why, and where he had died. I could only answer that they found his mangled body at Star Bend on October 17th.

She perked up. "I was at Star Bend the night before, and I saw someone there."

They showed detectives in movies chasing clues, but they don't describe how it really feels to learn something about a case you're working on. Maybe the excitement was because I'm related to the dead, but nonetheless I needed to know more. I didn't bother asking why she was there. I was sure it was related to her *work*.

She said two men got into a car. They appeared to have come from the forested area around Star Bend. I asked her to describe the car, and she went on to describe the car that Joel had waved at when we were having lunch. I'm not one hundred percent sure that it's the same car. I'm not very good with makes and models, but there was one thing that was different about this car. It was all black with tinted windows, very common in this area, but the trim was gold. She noticed this too as the car she was in lit up the trim as it drove by.

Don't trust Joel.

I felt that I couldn't trust anyone, even this girl that claimed Adam was her everything. So, I kept it all to myself despite her questioning eyes. I asked if that was everything she had seen, and she said they quickly got inside and sped off. She didn't catch a license plate and only had a vague description of the two men. I wrote it down, nonetheless.

Two very tall men, probably over six feet tall, one wearing a black hoodie and the other in a red hoodie.

They had to be Adam's killers. Or at least whoever dumped him off. It was then that I realized I should have gone to the crime scene sooner. It was then that I realized I didn't know much about this case. Was Adam killed on scene or somewhere else?

With nothing more to offer me, I left Chantelle's in a hurry, dropping off the chain and my phone number. I told her to call me if she had any more information to offer or if she needed a shoulder to cry on. I really only meant the first one.

I rode my bike to the police department, thanking the cool October weather. The detective's office was a wreck and I wondered how he ever got any work done or any cases solved. That's because he didn't. We spoke briefly before I got the feeling I wasn't going to get very far with him. He pulled out Adam's case file right in front of me but wouldn't show me any of the documents. This made me uneasy. He said it was top secret information, like I was some child. Little did he know I'm excellent at distractions and not afraid to break the law. I mean, I was in a police station with an unregistered gun in my pocket.

"We have no more information on Adam's case, but we're working as hard as we can."

I loved that the statement made me nauseous, as it set my plan into action. I turned away to cough, covering my mouth with my hand and slipping a finger down my throat. The icing on the cake was that the room smelled of turkey lunch meat, and as my finger hit my uvula, I saw the turkey sandwich sitting on his desk. Up came two dark cups of coffee onto the deep blue carpeting. He looked at me with wide eyes and rushed out of the room mumbling something about paper towels, clearly disgusted. I guess any chance of him finding me attractive is squashed. I snatched the file, shoved it into my bag, and ran.

Today was a successful day, but I know I have a limited amount of time with this thing.

I rode out to Star Bend and quickly photographed all the documents while sitting in this shithole parking lot.

Star Bend is a boat launch by the way. It sits on the backside of a community called Plumas Lake. That's where the uppity people live. The closest thing to a lake here is the Feather River, which is what Star Bend launches into. It's a dirty river that could kill you in a few minutes, but people like it here. Surrounding the parking lot is a forested area full of willows and cotton woods. This is where Adam's body was found. I'm probably sitting right where the killers were parked. Now to go through the paperwork while I still have it on hand.

[shuffling]

Sifting through this folder, I'm not learning much about Adam or his case. The first documents in here are actually his rap sheet, which is full of things I already knew about Adam.

Assault on a police officer, age 12.

That's a bit much considering the officer swung at him first.

Armed robbery, age 14.

Okay, first of all, he was *armed* with a butter knife, and the cashier almost shot him before a police officer inside the gas station detained Adam.

Moving on. There's something stuck to the back of his rap sheet.

[shuffling]

Oh.

Somehow the photograph of the crime scene isn't as bad as seeing him at the morgue. The blood looks fresh, so he had to have been killed then immediately dumped. It doesn't look like he was killed here. His hands were tied behind his back, a gag in his mouth, a blindfold over his eyes, and his feet were duct taped together. God, they filleted him with bullets. Based on his surroundings in the photo, I think I can find where he was at. They posted him up beside a really large stump.

The rest of the documents are useless. They haven't got a single suspect, and it doesn't look like they collected any DNA from Adam's body or his bindings.

So, it's off to see where Adam was dumped. Adam and I used to ride through here on our bikes. Speaking of, I need to lock mine up.

[click]

Okay, Adam really did love this place. We would hang out here often, which is why it's so tragic that they would dump his body here. In fact.

[leaves crunching]

The stump in the photo looks familiar, and if I'm not wrong, it's not too far from the path. Adam used to hop his bike up on this stump and hop off, something I never could learn. We had many lunches there, and–

And there are his initials, carved into the side. There's still police tape here, but the wind has blown it down into the dirt. His blood is still puddled here, but not enough to indicate he was murdered in this spot. It had to have happened somewhere else.

[wind noise]

I–I don't want to be here anymore. I feel sick and anxious. I came and saw what I needed to, now–now I have to leave.

Did the killers know he loved this place? Did they know he smoked his first joint on this stump? Or that he made everyone who came here carve their initials into the stump they laid his body next to? Or was it all a coincidence?

Don't trust Joel.

God, did Joel do it? Could Joel really be the one who dumped his best friend here? Joel is pretty tall, not over six feet, but he's at least 5'11. And he's got tons of hoodies. Could Chantelle have seen him? But why Joel?

We were arguing that night.

Could a spiff really have killed Adam? Something as small as an argument?

[leaves crunching]

Are those legs?

Oh my God, there's a body.

[click]

I called the police, but she was already dead. Looked to have been dead for a while. I recognized her as the butcher at a little Mexican mart down the street from our apartment building. Poor Sola. I noticed in recent years she looked to have been using, and now she suffered the same fate as Adam.

Her thin arms had been bound in orange rope, appearing to be the same as the rope that was found around Adam's wrists. Her body was bare of anything except shredded and bloodied underwear, and her feet were duct taped as Adam's were. From where her breasts used to be to her hips was shredded, and upon first looking at Adam's injuries, I believed it to be hundreds of bullet wounds, but I was wrong. The autopsy report was no help, simply stating his heart had been torn open. It didn't state by *what*, and I don't know how the coroner here hasn't been arrested for hindering a police investigation.

Looking at Sola's body gave me new insight. There were bullet wounds, but that wasn't what killed her. First, she had been ripped open. By the direction of the wounds on her body, which I'm currently comparing the photos I took of Sola and the photo from Adam's case file, they were laid on something, or something was laid on them, and it caught and pulled their flesh in one direction, like a giant chainsaw. The bullet holes appear on the surface of these tears.

Adam and Sola suffered greatly.

Could they be connected?

Their deaths were identical.

Now I need to know if she was using the same stuff this *Ricardo* was selling. And I have a plan to find out. The killers killed her just in the same way as Adam, and the officers on scene had *a lot* of obvious suspicion towards me.

I was smart enough to climb a tree and stash the gun in a hollow but forgot about the case file in my bag. There was a lot on my mind. A deputy found it and called over the detective I spoke to, who goes by Bill, as they were taking photos of Sola.

Lucky for me, something that made me guilty also alibied my reasoning for being at Star Bend. I was obviously curious about the case, and in their *kind hearts*, the officers decided to give me a warning and send me home. I was even escorted home in one of their SUVs, to the surprise of my parents who were out on the balcony when I arrived.

There's a lot spinning around in my head right now, so I need to just say it all.

Joel is definitely a suspect, and that hurts me to even *think* that.

I don't know as much about Adam as I thought, but maybe Chantelle does. She is an asset.

Adam—Adam suffered so much. He was ripped to *shreds* and the police don't care. The police are not my friends. I'm doing their job.

Mom and Dad are worried about me. They asked why I got escorted home, and I just told them I was too tired to bike home from the store. I don't think they believed me. I'm on thin ice.

I need to get Adam's gun from Star Bend. And soon.

I need to talk to Ricardo, but I'm not a hundred percent sure my original plan will work. I'm a local. Almost everyone here would recognize me, so I can't just go buy drugs from this guy.

But I know someone who can.

Yeah. Shit. I need to write this down. Chantelle may know Ricardo. Why didn't I ask her that? I'm still confused about something with her. I didn't see anything about them getting clean in the text messages. Maybe I'll read more. I don't think I can fully trust her yet, but she's the closest thing I've got to Adam's secret life right now.

Oh, and, last night Chuck asked if we could have lunch tomorrow. I said yes. I have to keep him close. He could fill in some of the blanks I've got. And I've got so many. Like what could have torn Adam open? That wasn't from getting run over, and I don't think any human could do that, even with a saw of some kind. Honestly, it made me think of how people get hung up in escalators, and then torn to shreds.

Yeah, it had to be a machine, right?

Shit. This is hard. I feel so useless. I haven't asked anyone the right questions. I haven't been timely with finding clues. All I have are these little pieces of string, and somehow, I have to piece it back into the rope that'll lead me to the killer.

Okay, that's dramatic, but I literally only have the description of a car and two anonymous figures. I don't know what or who killed Adam, or Sola for that matter. I know Adam had a new dealer, but who's to say if he's guilty? His best friend is—

His best friend is selling, too. Those pills, all those pills. I'm. So. Dumb.

Joel is selling the same stuff Ricardo is.

Or was Joel really Adam's new dealer?

I can't think straight. All the questions the officers asked me are still floating around in my head.

Why are you here?

Do you know this woman?

Where have you seen her before?

They're all so elementary. How can I solve this case if no one around me is trying?

It's late. I'm exhausted. Mom told me she has a surprise for me tomorrow. I can only imagine what it is. I hope to God it's not another cat. I hate cats.

At least I'll get to see Chuck tomorrow. Maybe he can help me make sense of everything.

Chapter Five: Confirmation

"Here Babs," Adam said, handing me the pipe. I took it carefully as it crackled. The image of the melting crystal was all my eyes could focus on. As I put it to my lips, the smoke hit my nostrils, burning all the way to my throat. I took a big hit, filling my lungs with fire. When I looked up to hand Adam the pipe, he was *dead*.

He wore the suit we buried him in. It had been torn open at some point, exposing a mess of dripping flesh. Sitting on his knees, like a child on Christmas morning, Adam's intestines lay sprawled out before him. He panted. A bloody heart beat from within his chest cavity, defying the way his face and skin screamed *death*. His glazed eyes met mine as his mummified hands reached for the pipe. Adam's body appeared as an amalgamation of fresh, living tissue wrapped in skin aged for centuries. Flakes of him landed in my hands in return for the pipe.

He put it to his wrinkled, dry lips, inhaling as smoke drifted from his punctured lungs. Adam laughed, that same smoker's laugh he had when he was alive, and his eyes rolled back in his head, leaving behind two black orbs.

Something pushed me, seeming to thrust against my shoulders, like two giant hands. I toppled over backwards, falling through darkness until I landed in a plush, leather recliner. Chantelle sat in front of me and spoke softly.

"Your brother was a good man."

Tears twinkled on her cheeks. We briefly spoke, mainly about Adam, before a thunderous crashing took my attention. Chantelle paid no attention to it as giant legs entered her apartment. I tried to look up but could only see up to the legs' leopard print thongs. Above them was a dark void.

She sobbed more, crying into her hands as the legs danced about us, gyrating their hips around. I couldn't focus on her words. My heart beat fast in my chest, the legs seeming to dance with its booming rhythm. I got up to run away, but the floor gave way underneath my weight. I found myself falling again, falling through nothing but black. I could feel the wind chill on my skin as I sped through this chasm.

Deeper and deeper I fell.

I was in Joel and Chuck's living room. I had no recollection of landing, but there I was. Mountains of pills surrounded me, each a different, pretty color. Joel beckoned me from the couch, waving me toward him with a wad of cash. I sat on the couch, and that's when Chuck appeared. He sprang up from a mountain of pills and grabbed me from behind. With cold fingers, he forced my mouth open and held me before Joel.

Joel carefully took a pill from the pile on his coffee table and gently laid it on my tongue as I struggled against Chuck. The pill dissolved, fizzing in my mouth and leaving my tongue to feel numb and tingly. Joel plucked another pill from the pile and set it on my tongue. Before it could dissolve, he picked and placed another, then another, and another.

Soon my mouth was full of pills, so many that my jaw cracked as it stretched over this hoard. They melted on my tongue, the taste and smell so overwhelmingly sweet. Joel tried to set another pill into my mouth, but it couldn't find a space and tumbled to the floor. He grunted, motioning something to Chuck.

I felt Chuck's grip tighten, his fingernails digging into the soft flesh of the roof of my mouth and below my tongue. He ripped outward, tearing my lower jaw from its hinge. Joel took handfuls and handfuls of pills, shoving them down my now exposed esophagus. I choked, coughing pills and a spray of blood into Joel's face, but it only hardened the look in his eyes. He gritted his teeth, shoving his hand directly into my stomach and letting go.

The pills filled my stomach quickly. I could hear myself crying, the pain in my jaw was immense, but as the pain in my stomach grew, I knew what was next.

I heard the ripping before I felt it, and as Joel shoveled in another handful of pills into my gullet, my stomach burst. Fiery pain shot through my body from my navel outwards. I looked down in time to see what I had birthed.

There sat a bloodied Mr. Chubbz, as crushed and putrid as he probably is now under Adam's coffin. His head lifted and swiveled to look at me, and out of his broken snout, he whispered,

"They're waiting for you."

Silence.

All of the pain subsided, and I hung in warm nothingness until a light shone before me. It approached me, crunching through leaves and sticks on its way. I saw myself, wielding a flashlight in a panicked state.

"Adam! Adam this isn't funny anymore!"

I had been there before. Looking for Adam as he hid in the forest. The river rushed by to my left. I swooped the flashlight that way, thinking I heard someone in the water.

"Adam, did you fall in?!"

From where I stood watching myself, I could see young Adam hiding in a bush not too far away. My younger self inched closer to the river, getting dangerously close to the steep bank. From my memory I knew in reality Adam came to my side, grabbing my shirt just as I slipped, and saving me from falling in.

I watched, breathless and unable to move as I fell into the murky depths. Adam laughed from his place behind the bush, and I noticed someone sitting beside him. He pulled out a lighter, striking it so the small flame illuminated his friend.

Sola sat beside him, just as pale and dead as the day I had found her. My screams were out in the distance, slowly fading beneath the sound of rushing water. Sola stood, approaching where I stood, where I assumed I could not be seen. Like a camera on a tripod, I could see but could not move. She got close, her nose pressing into what I assumed was my eye. She breathed heavily, the smell of skunk filling my nose and mouth. What I mistook for anger in her eyes was merely confusion as she began to cry. She mumbled things, until she finally yelled,

"Help us!"

She backed away from me, her body dismembering and disintegrating into the soil, and like every zombie movie out there, hands rose from the dirt, followed by bodies in various stages of decomposition. I recognized some from missing persons posters I had seen around town, others were without heads, or their faces were mutilated to the point I couldn't identify them. Each clawed their way from the earth and made their way to where I stood.

For the first time, when I looked down, I could see myself. I wore a big t-shirt and shorts, something I usually wear to bed. The bodies crawled up my legs and pulled me to the moist earth. I couldn't move, not that I would know where to go, and as they dragged me, I heard their whispers.

"Save us. Dear God, please save us."

They dragged me to a hole in the ground and shoved me in. I watched them bury me, feeling as dirt hit my unmoving eyes. I couldn't close them to shield myself from the earth that fell upon me, and slowly I felt the crushing weight of being buried.

I laid in the nothingness for some time, wondering what was to happen next. At this point, everything that had happened prior seemed like a blur. I didn't remember dead Adam, or the gyrating thongs, or giving birth to a zombified Mr. Chubbz. I only remembered one thing, and soon I was submerged in it.

"Happy birthday to you. Happy birthday to you. Happy birthday, dear Adam. Happy birthday to you!"

Joel leaned over, blowing out Adam's candles. Everyone gasped, but Adam kept smiling. He was young, missing a few teeth, and really didn't care. I felt strapped to my chair, unable to move as the two morphed in front of me. They aged rapidly, their skin wrinkling and flaking away before snapping back to teenage years.

"Try it, it won't hurt. I do it all the time," Joel said, handing Adam a pill, similar to the one he tried to give me. A smiling Adam took it, unbeknownst to my watchful eyes.

They morphed again, reaching death before snapping back to young adulthood.

"I'll drive you, buddy. We can pick up something fun on the way there," Joel said, wrapping an arm around Adam's shoulders and guiding him out of the house. Of course, he would drive, Adam couldn't keep a car without selling it off for…

For pills.

"Don't trust Joel."

I woke with a start, thinking I heard a gunshot. Up and off my bed, I stared out the window for ten minutes, only seeing Slim and a few ladies of the night, as my mother calls them, out in front of Smith's. I was shook, to my core. And with everything so vivid in my mind, I had to record the dreams. Not everything in them was fictional.

I never did drugs with Adam, and not only because I didn't want to, but because Adam never asked. When I would talk to him about his addiction, there was such guilt in him. It poured out of him in the most abstract ways. After we'd argue, there would always be a gift in my room. After he and my parents would argue, he would try to stay clean for what short time he could. And he rarely did it if I was around. I think that came down to pride, not just guilt.

And Adam had saved me from drowning, but only after playing a vicious game of hide and seek with me. Star Bend has always been a creepy place to me, with its droopy trees and its closeness to such a deadly river. Never did I expect it to become a dumping ground, much less for it to become the place they dumped my brother.

I hate this place.

I started to hate it when Adam started using. I always blamed living here for his addiction, but when I looked in the mirror, I knew it wasn't true. There were plenty of clean people here, and what I'm sure we all have in common is: we don't have an enabler. Joel's always been pushy. Pushing Adam to jump off a tree, resulting in him breaking his leg. Pushing Adam to try beer, then weed, then pills, and God knows what else. Joel acted like Adam was his sidekick. And maybe he was. Maybe Adam felt safe with Joel.

The note still hangs me up. Why would Adam write it but continue to be friends with Joel?

[click]

Jeez, it's only 3:45 a.m. I don't think I can sleep after all that. I actually *felt* the pain. My stomach has the lingering feeling you get after being in pain for a long period of time, like the absence of pain gives a tingly sort of feeling.

I think if anyone ever does find these recordings, they're going to think I'm crazy.

[click]

I think I'm going to go back to Star Bend, see what I can find, plus I need to get Adam's gun. What if there are others like Adam?

What if it's a serial killer?

I don't know about a serial killer here in Olivehurst, but I do know that the police aren't doing everything they can, especially Detective Bill.

I don't like him.

DNA is so advanced nowadays. Can't they just swab his body and find some DNA? A hair? Skin cells? A carpet fiber? Anything?

It feels like it should be so simple. Dead body, detective work, find the killer. But it's not. According to Chantelle, there were two people that dropped him. So, two killers? Or one and an accomplice? Or a hoard of other killers and they're just the cronies?

I still can't think of what they used to torture Adam. The thought makes me sick, that he suffered so long. Ripped to shreds.

It's sick.

And more people are going through it. I guarantee there are more bodies being eaten by maggots out there. Dads will fish, teenagers will fornicate, kids will play, all unbeknownst to the quiet bodies around them.

[silence]

Sometimes I wonder where Adam is. I've never been the type to believe in Heaven or Hell, but the idea of him sitting in a safe place, watching down on us is comforting. Maybe he'll be reincarnated. I think he'd want to be reincarnated as a dog. A golden retriever to be specific. He'd get to eat all the food he wanted and sleep all day. Yeah, it's easy to get lost in the what ifs; in the pleasant ideas that after death we get a second chance.

I think the best part of the Heaven idea is that the person can still hear you, that they are always with you, and you are able to communicate with them. You can think of them and say something to them and believe they heard you, but deep down in my heart, I know no one is listening.

If anyone was listening, Adam would have been able to get clean. He tried so many times. And I know damn well his death is related to his addiction. Who else would murder him but a vicious drug gang?

I'm just hurt, so hurt, because I know Joel is involved. If he's selling the same product as Ricardo, aren't they connected? Or am I dumb?

[paper shuffling]

Yesterday I wrote another letter to Adam. Whether he knows about it or not, I'd still like for it to exist, and I'd like to hear how it sounds.

"The note you wrote about Joel has been the most confusing part of all of this. Where does this mistrust come from?

I've been working day and night on your case. There's not a minute that goes by that I'm not thinking about finding your killer.

I found out about your girlfriend. She's just as distraught as I am.

I've been conflicted lately. Torn between being mad at your killers and you. Had you taken the rehab seriously one of the countless times we tried, you could still be here. You could have gotten a nice job, moved out with Chantelle, and started to work for the community.

We lowered you into your grave, Adam. You'll never be here again."

I feel guilty for the statement about being angry, but it's the truth. Clean Adam would have had no use for drugs or Joel or this street life that he led. He could have gotten out.

[click]

I fell asleep. This morning has been interesting to say the least. I forgot most of the dreams I had last night and had to listen to the recording to get a refresher. Wow is the only word that came to mind.

Again, I got up, had my coffee, and watched the news, only to be enraged to see Detective Bill on the screen. Lies spewed from his filthy mouth as he told the plastic-like news anchor that crime has gone down in Olivehurst. Two days ago, there was a homicide in one of the apartment buildings in my complex. *Lover's Quarrel* I had heard from a neighbor. And the day after that, there was a shooting at the Super Mart a few miles down the road.

Just where my mom pulled a few strings and got me a job.

Her old friend Jasmine works there. Jasmine and my mom got to talking one day, about how I'm a loner and I need to get out more. Jasmine suggested I start working there, and who am I to resist when they already got me a vest with my name on it?

Honestly, I'm not mad. My mom is looking out for my best interest, but Super Mart? I think I'm more of a CoffeeTime employee. Okay, in *all honesty*, I would have been happy to take the job had Adam not been murdered this week. Playing detective has made me feel like I have a purpose and that maybe I'm finally doing Adam right.

I start tomorrow, learning my section of the store and stocking shelves. The pay isn't bad for a job I can ride my bike to, and maybe now I won't go crazy pacing my room the times I don't know where to go. Not to mention, everyone I know goes to Super Mart, and it'd be great to do some surveillance *incognito*.

With nothing better to do, I decided to go to Star Bend, that was until I checked my phone.

Chuck canceled lunch today, saying he had to *work*. Last I remember he doesn't have a job.

Oh yeah, by the way, Chantelle is pregnant.

Believe me when I say I felt every emotion when I saw the text, and rather than texting back, I hopped on my bike and sped over to her apartment. She answered the door, this time fully dressed, and allowed me in.

I've never been the kind of person to hold things back so before she could even sit down, I asked, "Is it Adam's?"

She shrugged, a guilty look on her face. "I don't know."

I was almost mad, until I remembered her profession. "Well, how can we find out?"

She said the doctors could check, and she assured me that she uses protection every time she's with a *client*.

"How far along are you?"

"Three months."

"Did Adam know?" I was almost in tears, waiting for her answer like my life depended on it.

"No."

Oh, the spear that was thrusted into my heart.

Adam was what my father would call: a strange child. He'd often steal my baby dolls and rock them and feed them with the utmost care. My father wasn't one for it, but my mother saw it as a good sign that she'd get to care for grandchildren in the future. A baby would have changed everything for him. I think it would have been the turning point in his life that would keep him clean.

I sobbed, crying for a good ten minutes before I could get myself to stop and talk to Chantelle. She explained that she had just found out last night, and I was the first and only person she told.

"I don't expect you to help," she said, cautiously, "but I still wanted you to know."

I shook my head. "No, no, I'll do what I can to help," I said. I'm finally an aunt.

This new job was meant for Adam. This wonderful news was meant for Adam. This child was meant for Adam. Yet here I was, taking his place.

I feel the utmost guilt. I know the job was originally lined up for Adam, and I know Chantelle would have never told me had Adam still been here. I didn't even know she existed until he died.

What do they call it? Survivor's guilt? Only, I wasn't in the same accident as Adam. I feel as if I should have been in his place.

Chantelle told me she had some errands to run and ushered me out of her apartment. I rode my bike to Smith's, not wanting to go inside my place just yet, and outside I met Slim.

He said, "Hey, lil' Abigail, isn't it?"

I nodded, thinking of Adam's gun sitting in that tree hollow all the way at Star Bend.

"Yeah, yeah," he licked his dry lips before continuing, "Ricardo," he paused, glancing around, "he moved."

I shrugged my shoulders, playing dumb. "Who?" I asked.

"Ricardo. Adam's new dealer."

Oh, now the old man has something to say.

"Chantelle told me you lookin' for who killed Adam."

I nodded, remembering the story of how the two met.

"Only makes sense that it was Ricardo. Ain't no one else had a beef with that boy."

I nodded, staying quiet.

His eyes, wide as they already were, widened more. "Oh! But you didn't hear that from me."

I shook my head. "No, sir." I said and motioned that I zipped my lips. "Anything else you know?"

Slim scratched his arm and looked around, before leaning in real close. The smell of rotten fish and tobacco suffocated me until his words made me forget.

Joel is working for Ricardo.

Chapter Six: Dead Relatives

Confirmation! It was the confirmation I fucking needed!

I cannot believe out of all people, Slim was the one to be of value!

Well, in terms of the investigation. Uh. All people have value.

It was too late to do so, but I already planned on seeing Mama Maria *as soon* as I got off work the next day. All *night* I thought about it. I was so proud of myself. So, fucking proud. My hunch was right. And after sitting there, staring at the dark ceiling and feeling proud of myself for a while, I realized that I needed to actually *do* something with the confirmation.

So, this morning I got woken up by my mother. She insisted I wake up an *hour* before work despite me being able to be dressed and on my way in five minutes. The bike ride over would take around fifteen minutes, but that was a breeze. She combed my hair back and gave me something that pierced my heart as much as it pierced my skin. As I slipped on the blue vest, my mom came over with an enamel pin. She poked it through the vest, inevitably stabbing me. I winced, pulling the vest away to see a small spot of blood on my white t-shirt. She apologized, but I probably felt worse than she did.

The pin was of a skull, and it said "*Anxiety*" in squiggly letters.

My mind went back to the jean jacket in Adam's closet, the one covered in enamel pins.

Adam liked pins.

Adam suffered with anxiety since he was a kid.

Yet again I was dealing with confirmation, but this was not the sort that made me jump for joy. There was an instance where I was looking my mother in the eyes, and she was holding the pin, still stuck in my vest but pulled away from me. I stared deep into her dark eyes and almost called her out.

I almost said, "This job wasn't meant for me. It was meant for Adam."

But saying it in my head made me realize how dumb it sounded.

Of course, the job was for the one going through rehab; the one that was gone a lot; the one that stole just to get high.

I stayed home and read books. I had an interest in journalism. I never got in trouble. But with Adam gone, I guess my mom thought it could help me. I think she's seen me struggle. I've been out of the house a lot, hanging out with people I never would have if Adam was still around. I know she cares, I just wish she would show it in other ways.

I gently took the pin from her and snapped it in place just below my name tag. Touching it, I thought of Adam's chest; how it would never rise and fall again; how it would never embrace anyone ever again; how he would never live again.

I grabbed my mom and forcefully hugged her, hot tears already rolling down my cheeks. She told me everything would be alright. I knew that was a lie. I may be here, healthy as can be, breathing this cigarette smoke infested air and eating a gas station burrito, and I may be able to walk the streets and smile, but deep down I'm broken.

I'll never get to know him.

I know you'll listen to this, whoever you are, and you'll say, "Well, she knew him pretty well I'd say." But as the girl that lived it, I don't think I do.

Growing up, across the hall from us was a family exactly like us. A mom, a dad, a sister, and a brother. They even had a cat that later inspired Adam's need for one. The brother and sister were similar in age as well and about five years older than us.

I hung out with the girl sometimes while Adam and her brother played ball. She'd always ask me questions about Adam, and I never knew the answers.

"What's his favorite color?"

I shrugged my shoulders. "I don't know."

She—by the way, her name was Cathy—so Cathy would gawk at me and answer the question about her own brother.

"Well, Timmy's favorite color is pumpernickel. I know because we tell each other *everything*."

I was jealous, so I started asking Adam questions. Mind you, we were around seven and eight years old.

"Adam, what's your favorite color?"

He was standing in the kickball field at school when I asked. He ignored me, calling to one of his friends instead. So, I asked again.

He quickly turned to me and shoved me down, spitting, *"Don't ask me things."*

I was wounded to say the least, and from then on, I was a background character in his life. Occasionally I took precedence in his mind, but then again it was about as often as a person thinks about their mailman. That's why the note and the gun surprised me so much.

I know he cared. It was a given.

"We're brother and sister," right?

Yeah. I may not have known his favorite color, but I knew he hated to leave me anywhere alone. Something about me being alone bothered him. Shit, sometimes I think he would have taken me into the bathroom with him if he wouldn't have been called a weirdo. He could be clingy at times, but he wouldn't speak in these moments.

Like sitting beside me while I read. Or bringing his lunch over to my table only to ignore all my questions and eat in silence. Or even temporarily stealing my things just so he could see me.

Maybe he was trying to emulate a cat's behavior, to be there and not speak and not address the other person.

As a teenager I learned that he listened to what I said, even my mumbling. I'd been upset that no one got me a candy gram for Valentine's Day. I thought for sure that a boy I liked would have gotten me one, but there I was, without one. Adam must've overheard me telling Mom, but he said nothing.

When I got home from the library that night, there it sat on my bed, a stolen candy gram that was meant for a *Melisa*. It wasn't remotely close to Abigail, and it wasn't for me, but I indulgently ate it with a broken heart.

So, there was the pin on the chest of the vest meant for Adam.

There was a light mist in the air, and it caught up as dew drops on my sweatshirt as I sped past traffic in the bike lane. The dying trees around me reminded me that it's close to Halloween, the only holiday Adam really took part in. I rode my bike into the Super Mart parking lot, wondering if the cashier with no teeth was going to be the one showing me around today.

It wasn't. A very tall, black man saw me waiting by the cash registers when I first arrived, and he introduced himself. The first thing out of my mouth was,

"Is my bike okay locked up out front?"

His eyes widened, and he shook his head. So, the first thing we did was move my bike into the break room. I already had a good feeling that I would be looked after here.

His name is Jamal, and he's super sweet. His height had me taken aback, and when I asked how tall he is, he said he's six-seven. That's a whole foot and a half taller than me. He explained that he's the manager and if I have any questions or problems, to go to him. I'm glad the manager isn't the toothless lady. She's always rude.

I got the produce section and wished I wouldn't have left my sweatshirt in the break room. Jamal's hair distracted me while he showed me how to stack the bell peppers. He has a streak of grey in his tight, black curls, reminding me of the bride of Frankenstein. I couldn't say this of course, fearing he might not like the reference, but I did wonder if he'd ever been electrocuted.

He talked about a lot while he watched me load new rolls of bags on the dispensers and unload sacks of baby carrots. He spoke of his family, saying he had a daughter similar in age with me. I told him I remembered her from high school. She was another girl at the top of the class. Very quiet and reserved as well. If it wasn't for my shyness, I would have tried to be friends with her.

He smiled and told me she's dead.

Jamal didn't say it exactly like that. He said she temporarily moved to Nevada to go to college and had been one of the victims of a mass shooting.

It was everything in me not to cry. I said, "Oh, I'm sorry for your loss. She was a wonderful person," but it felt so forced.

I could see the tears in his eyes, and he said, "Thank you. I'm sorry for the loss of your brother."

We stared at each other in silence for a minute before a customer interrupted us. It was then that I knew Jamal is someone to keep around.

We had lunch together, and he told me that I'm a fast learner and that he usually has to spend at least a week training people. I told him it was just stacking vegetables.

He said, "Don't let anybody else hear you say that! They'll have you in here working for free!"

I laughed. Luckily, we had moved past the sadness of our lost loved ones and gotten into lighter topics.

He talked about his other daughter. She was much younger than I, and what he called an "uh-oh child." She had just started kindergarten this year, and he was happy for her, but also scared. He had been bullied in school a lot, but she seemed to be making friends left and right.

One thing he asked stuck with me.

"You still live with your parents?"

I nodded.

"Good. Good. Stay with them as long as they'll let you."

I think my parents planned for Adam and me to live with them in that apartment the rest of their lives. Adam wasn't into girls, well, we thought that at least, and I'm not into people in general. I don't think the idea bothered them. My mother always worried she would end up like her grandmother, dying alone in an old folks' home. I told her I would never do that to them, and I will keep that promise until I die.

So, after lunch I was out on the floor alone. Jamal said I had it together, and they needed a hand up front. Not too long after, a man I barely recognized came in, eyeing the fruit juice section.

I asked if he needed any help, and when he turned to look at me, my heart stopped.

Dark eyes narrowed on me, his brows knitting together in a V. A deep scar ran from the inner corner of his eye, across his cheekbone, and to his jawline.

Ricardo.

I had never met him. Didn't know what he looked like. And had no reason to believe this man was him, but I *knew* it was him.

His expression sweetened, and he said that he was looking for a drink his daughter would like. I'm not ashamed to say I had a vision of murdering this man's daughter. I would do it in front of him if I knew he killed Adam.

I pasted on a smile and showed him the strawberry banana drink.

"Can't go wrong with something sweet."

He grabbed it and thanked me. The smell of cigarette smoke wafted around him as he left to look at the mangos.

When I thought it couldn't get any worse, Detective Bill walked in. I was angry, but I was at work. It was my first day, and I couldn't risk anything, so I dove behind a rack of bread fresh out of the bakery. Bill walked with such confidence for such a scrawny man. I feel as if I could snap him in half if I so wanted to.

He approached the mangos, acting like he was looking at them whilst whispering to Ricardo. I desperately wanted to hear what they were saying, but as they whispered back and forth, the intercom came on, screeching the day's deals into everyone's ears.

I saw a wad of bills slip from Ricardo's pocket into Bill's hand, and right there I wanted to call them out. I wanted to scream *Killers!* so everyone in the store would know.

Adam didn't matter to Bill because his killer was paying him. Crime doesn't exist when the police are on the payroll of the drug lords.

Detective Bill left, a sick smile on his face. I crouched down behind the bread and softly cried into my hands.

I was really alone in this investigation.

Toward the end of my shift Chuck came in. He saw me and his grim face turned into a goofy smiling one. I guess he didn't know I was starting a new job here, and my plan to not tell him was foiled on the first day.

First thing out of my mouth was, "How was work yesterday?"

His eyes widened, and he looked like a ventriloquist doll with no puppet master. Then he smiled. "It was good."

I nodded, stacking jalapenos. Mama Maria taught me to always wear gloves when dealing with peppers, so there I was wearing produce bags on my hands to stock the jalapenos.

Chuck asked when I would be getting off work. I told him I only had a few more minutes, and he said he'd wait.

I'd wanted to talk to Jamal some more, see how he was doing, but also didn't want Chuck to wait on me. He did his shopping while I finished up and clocked out. He was a nice guy, I guess, and I was glad to have someone around to talk to.

As we walked out of the store together, me dragging my bike along, I thought of all the things I could tell him. I didn't think it was right of me to tell him about Chantelle. It really wasn't my business to tell anyone. And I desperately wanted to tell someone about Detective Bill, but… could I trust him?

He put his arm around my shoulders as we walked in the direction of my apartment, and I let him. So, instead of bringing our moods down entirely to talk about the investigation, I talked to him about Jamal. I told him that I really related to him, and it was sad to hear that such a smart girl with a bright future had passed. I even confessed how bad I felt that I was glad someone else knew my pain. Everyone that knew Adam of course had been through the pain, but this man was off in his own life and wasn't connected to us. From the moment we met, we could sympathize with each other.

Chuck quickly changed the subject.

I looked up at him when he abruptly changed the topic to the weather. I couldn't believe how disconnected he was. It was like he didn't care.

I asked him why he did that, and he looked at me with a stupid innocent look, and said, "Did what?"

I scoffed and pulled away from him, hopping on my bike. I rode off, yelling back, *"Call me when you care!"*

When I got to my apartment steps after furiously pedaling, I realized Chuck was jealous. It wasn't a thought I came to realize naturally, but my mother's voice called out in my mind and said, *"He's just jealous."* She always told me things like that about guys, so it was believable that she would say something like that, and honestly it was believable that Chuck was jealous. I shook my head and hauled my bike up the stairs, only to remember I was going to Mama Maria's after checking in with my parents.

I sighed, pulling the bike with me.

As I was walking to my apartment, I saw Adam. He was walking away from me, but everything about him screamed *Adam!* His close-cut hair, baggy shorts and big t-shirt even though it was freezing out. Even his shoes looked like the pair Adam frequently wore.

My voice caught in my throat. I wanted to speak out as tears flooded my eyes.

What if he turned around and wasn't Adam?

What if he was?

My nose burned, so I sniveled, and the man turned around.

The illusion was broken as his face resembled no person I had ever seen. I dove into my apartment, not wanting to be under the eyes of this stranger.

I checked in with my parents, letting them know I was off to see Mama Maria. My mom asked why, and I hadn't thought of an answer to give her. When I didn't answer, she turned from the stove for the first time since I had been home and saw the mix of tears and mist on my face. The tip of my nose was bright red from the cold, and I think it gave the impression that I had cried more than I really had. She patted me on the shoulder and told me to go, even gave me a box of chocolates to give Maria.

As far back as I can remember, Joel has confessed *everything* to his mommy. He and Adam couldn't get into *anything* without her knowing.

"Mommy, we took some cookies from the cookie jar," he'd say, pouting.

Adam would look at him, dumbfounded. I would snicker as I never got a share of the loot, but Maria didn't care anyway. She'd shrug it off and say, "That's okay, hijo."

Mama Maria is *very* Catholic, and if we got stuck at her house on a Sunday, you bet your ass we were stuck going to church with her and her children. In my time there, I saw a handful of people go to confession, and I think that's where it all started for Joel.

His mother was his 24/7 confession booth.

She answered the door and quickly let me in, making a hot chocolate for both of us and setting a chair by the fireplace for me. Once she was settled into her recliner, I did the normal thing, asked how she was doing, gave her the chocolates. She said she was well, and I could see she was curious why I had come over.

When there was a lull in the conversation, and we were all up to date on each other's whereabouts, I hit her with it.

"My mom got me this job at Super Mart. It's pretty boring." I waited a second as she smiled and nodded, then *bam*. "What does Joel do for Ricardo?"

Her eyes widened to the size of saucers. Ah, I could have laughed, but I didn't. I couldn't.

She must have said *uh* five times before I interrupted her.

"I heard he got a job working for him, and it's got to be better than stacking fruits all day." I laughed, but Maria didn't laugh with me.

After a few seconds of awkward silence and staring, she said, "Ricardo is the manager at Soki."

Soki.

There's always a front in movies. Ah, the laundry mat? The only laundry there is money laundering. The mechanic shop?

The one on Oak Lane? The only thing they're fixing is sports games. Okay, but you get the point.

Soki is a fruit drink manufacturer. Huge warehouse. Lots of space for lots of *things*.

Yet again, *confirmation*. She has confirmed Joel is working for this man, and now I know *where*.

I could have left then. That was all the information I needed, but I thought *why not try one last thing?*

I said, "Oh, that's cool. What does Joel do there?"

She was prepared for this one, and said, "He's a line worker, but he's hoping to move up to supervisor soon."

I nodded. "Do you think I should apply?"

Maria smiled, and said, "I think so. What days are you off?"

I was surprised to say the least. "I'm part time right now, so I'm off tomorrow."

She said, "I'll have Joel pick you up tomorrow morning so you can apply."

I've never been more terrified in my life.

Chapter Seven: Abomination

My parents were proud of me this morning. They think I'm finally taking charge of my life by scouting out a second job. My mom told me to take it easy, not to overwork myself, and my dad patted me on the back, a sure sign that he's proud of his little girl.

I'm glad they didn't know I was walking into the lion's den.

I waited out on the second-floor balcony, chatting with my neighbor. Martha's a good woman. Older. Never had kids. But she'd give the shirt off her back despite the hardened look of her face. Oh, and she smokes like a freight train.

I tried to keep the conversation light, wanting to quell my jitters. I almost reached over and snatched the cigarette from betwixt her fingers. I would have inhaled all of it in one drag, but I'm not much of a smoker.

Joel's car rolled into the parking lot, so I said my goodbyes and ran down the stairs, hoping this was not my last day on earth.

I couldn't bring my gun with me. I was fearful that someone would find it, and I didn't need another reason to be scared. Not to mention it still sat in the hollow of a tree in Star Bend.

Hopefully.

Getting in Joel's car, I wish I had a camera. He was just as nervous as I was, and we gave each other the exact sheepish smile before he pulled out into traffic.

"How are you today?" he asked.

He never asked how I was doing. It boosted my confidence to know he was nervous, too, and I was curious why he was so nervous.

"So, you started working?" he asked, as if *he* didn't just start *working* recently.

I told him how Mom got me a job at Super Mart and when I heard he was working for Soki, it intrigued me.

"*Why?*" His knuckles were white on the steering wheel.

I said, "Because if you're willing to tie yourself down to a job, it must be worth spending time at."

He instantly relaxed, even smirked a bit.

"Yeah, I've never been the committing type," he said.

I thought, *only been the committing crimes type.*

By the time we got to the Soki warehouse, we were both somewhat at ease and at the very least, we were more relaxed than we were when I first got in the car.

Joel skipped the customer parking lot, then even skipped the worker's parking spaces. He drove around back and parked alongside some very nice, *all black,* cars. We got out and he led me to a door, letting me go in first.

I gasped.

A sweet odor hit me square in the face, and Joel laughed.

He said, "Yeah, it takes a while to get used to that."

Joel walked in around me, guiding me down a hall. I had never seen him dressed so nicely. There was no way he was working on the line. I figured he must have an office in here somewhere and that Mama Maria lied. He knocked on a door and waited a second.

A gruff voice said, "Come in."

I knew I would have to see Ricardo again. I knew it. But it didn't stop me from being scared. Something in me is convinced he killed my brother, and if he wasn't the one to do the damage, he was at least there to orchestrate it.

When Ricardo saw me, his face lit up.

"Ah, the nice girl from Super Mart. What are you here for?" he asked with a large smile. I know he knows my name.

Joel answered for me, and there began the awkward hiring process that I knew wasn't professional, but very typical in small towns. Just look how I got a job at Super Mart. The conversation went from me to Joel to Ricardo, from Ricardo to me to Joel, and on and on and on. I felt as if maybe they were waiting for me to crack. Like they thought I was going to slip up and say I was there hunting for clues about my brother's death.

Finally, I mentioned it.

Ricardo asked me why I wanted to work there for the tenth time. That may or may not be an exaggeration, but I answered with:

"Well, ever since my brother's death, I've been cooped up in the house. My mom got me a job at Super Mart, but it's only part time. I just," here I paused for a sigh, "I just don't want to be home anymore."

Ricardo's eyes softened. My original answer was I was looking for more money, but I think they both knew it was something more than that, so I made it more than that. I saw the picture of Ricardo and his three daughters on the wall. They looked to be 10, 14, and one close to my age, so I ground it in with:

"His room is right across from mine, so I can't have my door open anymore." I felt real tears sprout in my eyes. It was tragic but exactly what I needed. "And my window overlooks the liquor store, and that was the last place he had gone to before he went missing." I frantically wiped away the tears, acting as if I was embarrassed. Joel stepped forward and had the audacity to put an arm around my shoulders. I continued: "I've been shutting myself in my room and staring at the ceiling for days." Ricardo's eyes watered, so I put my arm around Joel, and ended with, "Luckily friends like Joel have been keeping me company, and when I found out he was working here, I figured it would help to have a friend in my workplace."

Ricardo nodded, clearing his throat, and offered me a position at the front desk. Their last clerk had been fired and even a part time clerk was better than none. I asked if he was really okay with it being part time, stating that I could quit the Super Mart job, and he assured me it was *perfect*.

A knot formed in my stomach, but Ricardo graciously showed me to my desk.

It was in utter disarray. He said the last clerk had *disappeared*, and he hadn't been able to find a replacement, so all the paperwork had started piling up. My first responsibility was to clean the desk and organize all the papers on top of it. Ricardo patiently explained what forms were for what and what to do with them while Joel stood by with a watchful eye.

Ricardo's final words were, "If you find a USB, give it to me *immediately*. Do not plug it in and wa-look at what's on it."

Well, obviously it had video on it. Ricardo's little slip had my curiosity piqued. I nodded, but knew if I found it, I would watch it.

The desk was a *wreck*, but I had it cleaned in under an hour. Sorted all the files and forms and paperwork like a pro. I got to the last bit of garbage, throwing out any sticky notes I thought weren't of importance. The old clerk's name was Wanda. She had adorable handwriting, but she wrote notes for everything.

The USB had been sitting under one of Wanda's fifty million sticky notes. I saw it, made eye contact with it, and my heart raced.

What could be on it? What would I be watching?

I almost laughed when I thought it could be a sex tape of Ricardo. If I thought a video condemning him to the murder of my brother would be great for blackmailing, I could only imagine the power of a sex tape.

So, I snatched it before anyone came strolling through the doors or from the hall. Earlier I'd seen a brand-new pack of three USBs in the drawers somewhere, so I grabbed one and shoved the packaging with the other two deep into the trash.

At this point I thought, it was either chance death or risk ignorance, so I copied the files from the first USB and into the next, making sure that *all* the files remained on the first USB. There were so many videos, and all the thumbnails were black.

Ignorance is bliss, isn't it?

I watched as the files slowly uploaded and almost prayed to keep people away. I'm surprised that Ricardo would trust me with so much. I thought maybe it was nothing. I thought maybe it *was* a sex tape, a lot of them. I didn't expect to see what I saw.

The day passed in agony as I waited with that second USB in my shoe. I filled out my own paperwork, as well as three other new hires they had. I was told by a man delivering boxes of paper that Soki is growing fast. I think he saw how many people were waiting in line to be helped and was only trying to make a polite statement. It really only irked me.

Of course a front is growing as quickly as addiction is in America.

So, this whole time I have been under the impression that Ricardo is the top dog.

Boy, was I wrong.

I waited a while after uploading the USB before giving Ricardo his. I wanted to get rid of my jitters before approaching him with it. He smiled and thanked me saying, "I knew you'd give it to me right after finding it. Where was it?"

I lied and told him it was under the keyboard. I even gave a fake laugh and said, "Had I not spilled the jar of paperclips, I never would have found it!"

I think I've gotten pretty good at lying.

I walked back to my desk, preparing myself to organize the files Wanda saved on the desktop, which were sure to be a *mess*, but instead, I was greeted with a hoard of men. One of them was obviously of more importance than the others as they seemed to crowd around him. He was short, much shorter than even the next shortest man in the room. Even with his small stature, he appeared to know his presence.

Ricardo came out from his office in a hurry, his loud, quick footsteps only muffled by the thunderous machinery outside the door to my left.

They spoke in Spanish, of which I only know a few words, and they were mainly food items learned from Mama Maria. None of the words I heard pertained to food. The only word I recognized was:

Muerte.

It seemed to be directed at Ricardo, that was until I heard Joel's name.

The small man directed his sharp gaze at me, so I pretended to be busy typing on the computer. I ended up typing out some gibberish into a blank email that is probably still in my drafts.

Ricardo was sweating *bullets*. He wrung his hands around themselves and nodded after every word this small man said.

It was astonishing to see such a brutal looking man worn down to a nervous, submissive pet. He clung to every word, like his life relied on it, and I realized it probably did.

That was when the smaller man pointed at me. I looked to him, stunned. Ricardo jumped to my desk, putting a hand on my shoulder. He spoke very quickly, still in Spanish. My heart raced as I wondered whether my life was on the line.

The man walked over under the eyes of everyone in the room. He smiled and reached over the desk, taking my hand, and said,

"Hello, I'm Saul, the owner of this plant. Nice to meet you."

His smile was soft, but his eyes were vacant of any life. I shook his cold, calloused hand and wondered if he could feel how terrified I was. Saul nodded when I answered with my name. I omitted my last name, introducing myself as Abby. He and his men followed an almost trembling Ricardo down the hall and out of my range of hearing.

It was just about time for me to clock out when Joel came up behind me and laid a hand on my shoulder. I'd been absent-mindedly reading an email for the third time and didn't hear him approach, so his touch made me jump. I think he did it on purpose. He told me to clock out a few minutes early so we could get on the road.

As I grabbed my things, I thought about the USB in my shoe. I had done a bit of walking around with no problem but walking all the way to his car and up the stairs to my apartment was sure to be an issue. I told him I had to pee first, and he was clearly irritated and ushered me to hurry. As I peed, I slipped the USB out from my shoe, and tucked it safely into a pad that I then tucked into the pouch I have for all my pads and panty liners, then that went into my purse. I hoped that Joel would have no reason to ask for a pad.

When I looked up from my purse, I spotted a small table in the stall. On the table was a bottle of air freshener and a pump of lotion, but the thing that caught my attention was the box of tissues beside those. It was black and shiny. Most tissue boxes are brightly colored and made of cardboard. I feared that if I stared too long, I would spot a red LED light. So, I quickly pulled up my pants, washed my hands, and left with a sick feeling in my gut.

Joel's car stunk of cigarette smoke. I wondered what he had done all day, considering Mama Maria's "oh, he's a line worker" statement was clearly a lie.

He took the long way home, avoiding the freeway and driving me through farmland. I mainly stared down the ditch on the side of the road and wondered how many decomposing bodies were in there. I wondered if any were from the hands of Joel or Ricardo. Just as I turned to stare at Joel, he spoke up.

Maybe I'm becoming my mother, reading too much into things, but I think Joel killed Adam. I'm almost certain, as he said,

"I just want to apologize about your brother."

That was all he said. Nothing more. I nodded, and he turned back to driving. What was he supposed to apologize for? Other than being the one to start his addiction. What was there for him to be so sorry for?

And for him to address Adam as *your brother.* What a strange thing for him to do. If the roles were reversed, it would be no issue for Joel to address me as "your sister" to Adam, as we weren't close, but for him to do so for Adam, was strikingly odd.

I clutched my purse tightly and kept my mouth shut the entire drive, and as I clambered out of his car into my apartment's parking lot, I felt like I could breathe again.

He drove off without a word, and I wondered where I was going to watch the USB. We have no laptop or desktop, and I don't have a USB converter for my phone. As I got to the top of the stairs, I realized there was only one option.

The TV.

My dad frequently brought home USB drives with newer movies. He said he got them from his friends, but hey, not my business. So, he has a small USB reader hooked up to our TV. Only problem was finding some alone time. I really didn't want to launch a porn file of Ricardo in front of my parents, but deep down I knew there would be something much darker on this drive.

I walked in, expecting my parents to ask how it went, only to find a dark, empty apartment. The sun was setting, and my heart shuddered as I wondered where they were.

A note on the kitchen counter provided all the details I would need. They were over at the neighbor's apartment to play cards, and usually their sessions lasted until at least three a.m.

I had time.

You know what else I had?

Apprehension.

And lots of it.

A suspicious USB from a very suspicious organization, and I got a front row seat to its contents in my pitch-black living room.

All alone.

I was tempted to call Chuck, to see if he would come watch with me. Then I realized how *romantic* he would find the setting. *Oh, a darkened room and mysterious tapes to watch together? She must be courting me!*

I don't know, I just think that's something he would think. So, I sat on the couch as the USB loaded and clutched the pillow beside me with a white knuckled fist.

A scream.

A scream like no other I had ever heard filled our apartment. My eyes were frozen onto the screen. I found myself unable to tear myself from the image.

A woman hung from ropes bound around her ankles and wrists behind her back. She was slowly being lowered onto a conveyor belt. The usual smooth surface had been removed and replaced with jagged chains. It moved much faster than any conveyor belt I had ever seen. Two men moved into the scene from out of frame. Each wore plastic suits, like painters. The only thing I could see about either of them was where their eyes peeked out from behind their goggles.

The woman screamed, begging for her life, and I was finally released from my terror for a few seconds. I scrambled for the remote, hoping to turn it down before the neighbors heard.

The two men grabbed her by her elbows, and as she came nearer to the conveyor belt of doom, I realized what they were about to do. They braced their hands on her back and forced her down into the raucous teeth. They held her steady as the metal thrashed into her skin, tearing it free and carrying it away. Blood ran down to the floor, creating puddles of crimson to contrast against the white linoleum. She wailed, until those wails turned into gurgles. With each pass of the conveyor, the floor grew darker and darker. I watched in horror as the two men pressed their weight down onto her back, and her writhing slowed to a stop. I heard her take her last gasping breath, something that must have been autonomous, for she was far gone.

The video cut out. I could finally hear how I was panting in those few seconds of silence and darkness.

The next video began.

He screamed so loud. I'd never heard him scream like that before. Adam, in nothing but a pair of shorts, hung above the conveyor. It was clean, and the floor below it shone like a pearl. The two men approached him from out of frame. I was about to watch my brother die.

Finally, Adam formed words out of his screams.

"I can pay you all the money you need if you just let me go. *Please*."

Money?

"*Please*. My family needs me."

I waited for the men to call him a drug addict, to tell him his family didn't need him. Only the hum of the conveyor met his words, and I think that was worse.

He cried as they lowered him down, and I cried with him.

Money. It was all for money. I knew his addiction would kill him, but I always assumed it would be an overdose. He was only inches from the fast-moving teeth when the front doorknob jiggled. I shut the TV off and laid on the couch. My parents were home earlier than expected.

They crept inside. I could hear them tiptoeing around.

My mom whispered, "She must be in bed. Must have been a long day."

She sounded happy, like she was proud of me.

When the light flicked on, they both gasped, and someone shut it off quickly. Tears threatened to force their way between my closed eyelids, and I trembled as I kept them back. Mom and Dad went into their room and shut the door.

I sobbed, crawling off the couch. I wept silently as I removed the USB from the port and sailed into my bedroom. I wanted to smash the USB, but it was the only proof I had, not that the police here would help. In bed, I tossed and turned. I think I may have fallen asleep for fifteen minutes, but I woke in a cold sweat.

I wanted to talk to someone about it, or at least tell you, but I couldn't speak. I could barely breathe. Sometime after one a.m. I fell asleep, but here I am, at two-thirty, awake as ever.

I just—

Money?

Paper that the government prints on was worth my brother? Was worth all those people on that USB?

I—

I have no words.

Chapter Eight: Confession

Recorded The Night of October 28th

"*To Adam,*

I feel as though everyone around me has tried to set me in your place. Like I lived my entire life just to replace you when you died. I don't think it's possible, but that's how it feels.

Mom gave me the job that I know was meant for you.

Dad called me Champ the other day, a nickname I know he reserved only for you.

Chantelle texts me nonstop, like she has no one else. I know you were her everything, and I'm trying to help her through this, but I'm only the kid's aunt. I could never take the place of his father or teach him the things you could.

Chuck has been on my case lately, and Joel has been distant yet closer than ever.

I'm not you, Adam. I could never be you, and I hate that all these people are putting me in the place you rightfully should have been in.

Had I died, you would have grieved as yourself. No one would have tried to put you in my place, but that's a given I suppose. I see the pain everyone is going through. It's all valid, and, like I said, I'm doing the best I can, and I'm only one person.

When I'm not having nightmares, I dream of you. I dream of the life you could have had. We could have had. A life where you introduced us to Chantelle, and we accepted her with open arms as you two went to rehab. As you two found jobs and a life together and brought another Drummer into this world.

Would life have gone that way had you not died? There's no telling. But in my dreams, I like to pretend. I like to pretend that the world is perfect and that you're still here. That I never had to imagine you dying. That I never had to see you die.

The coroner's eyes still haunt me. The look he gave me before flicking the sheet away and exposing your cold body still gives me chills. He was wrong for that.

I hope whatever debt you had didn't carry on to whatever afterlife there may be. I hope you are resting easy.

[sniffle]

I hope that last part doesn't make him feel guilty if there's any chance he might have heard that. It's the truth though. Every waking minute I think of him. And every night I dream of him. To think of his body rotting in the ground makes me sick. His face haunts me.

Went to work today. Less chilly than the other morning, which was nice, all except the sweat stains under my armpits. Reminder: don't wear grey to work. In all honesty, I was excited to see Jamal. I feel like I can relate to him without him being too close to the situation. I can say how I feel without the guilt of putting more weight on him. He says how he feels about his daughter. I say how I feel about Adam. And that's that. No tears. No shared memories of the lost loved one to pore over.

When Jamal greeted me with a black eye, I was furious. A thousand questions must have poured out of my mouth before he finally got me to shut up. We hid away in the breakroom, and he told me someone had slashed his tires, waited at his car, and beat him up as he tried to leave work the night before. Jamal is tall but not very meaty. I could easily see someone beating him up, especially if they surprised him. He told me that he couldn't tell who his assailant was as they wore a bandana over their face, but he said they told him one thing.

"Stay away from her."

For a moment I wondered if he was seeing a woman that he wasn't supposed to, but the look in his eyes said all I needed to know.

She was *me*.

I wondered if Jamal was mad at me, if he thought it was my fault. If he did, he didn't show it. He helped me in the produce section, seeming to not want to leave me alone. Or maybe it was that he didn't want to be alone. He talked about his daughter a lot, and although I had the urge to talk about Adam, I let Jamal have his time. At lunch, he bought me a sandwich, and we sat together. I found myself thinking about the letter I wrote to Adam, and realized Jamal is placing me in a spot not too far away from his daughter's place.

I could never, ever fill it, but this sort of companionship reminds me of my own dad, and I'm sure Jamal misses these moments with his daughter.

I couldn't help but stare at his eye sometimes. Poor dude got it, that's for sure. Even now, sitting on my bed watching people crowd in front of Smith's in the dark, I can't think of who would do that to him.

After lunch, Jamal introduced me to other departments. He had done this on the first day, but I think he has hopes that I'll become a supervisor below him. He told me I have *"potential."*

I was having a grand old time, laughing at some joke Carl in home decor had said when a familiar face passed by.

Chuck glared at me when he walked by. I thought we had made eye contact, but he kept walking. Then he swung back around the other end of the aisle Jamal, Carl, and I were on. Again, I thought he was glaring at me as he sped by. The *third* time proved that he was in fact staring at Jamal. I waved at him this time, and it was like I wasn't there. And by the fourth time, I had to say something.

I stepped away from my coworkers, and by the time Chuck was creeping by the fifth time, I was there to snatch his arm.

"You're not very good at sneaking around," I said, dragging him away from where Carl and Jamal were.

He looked at me, aghast, as if he hadn't just made the most blatant move *ever.* I asked him what he was doing. He said he was just shopping, so I snatched up his right hand, peering down at his knuckles. No cuts. No bruising.

He reeled his hand away from me, asking me what I was doing. I told him my friend had been punched, and he had nothing to say.

"Ah, jeez, I'm sorry to hear that."

Chuck loves to play dumb, but I'm tired of playing, so I asked him what he was doing last night. He said he was out with the boys, something I can't fact check since I am not *one of the boys*.

Again, maybe I'm reading too much into things, but it seems kind of suspicious to me.

I looked down at Chuck's cart to see exactly what he was *shopping* for. Staring back at me was a teddy bear and a box of condoms.

I laughed. Oh, and I mean *laughed at* him. That's when it hit me that we were standing in the candle aisle. I guess Chuck had romance on the mind.

So, I asked him, "Aw, were you embarrassed to see me? Who's the special lady?"

Chuck is a ginger. And if you think a ginger's face is always red, you should see when they blush. He turned beet red and started stumbling over himself.

When I heard the words from his mouth, I about *fell out*. "Uh–you."

A teddy bear and condoms for me?! From Chuck?!

Who does this man think he is?

Uh, hi, hello, I know your brother just died, and you've been on the lookout for his killer, but I was just curious, if maybe, I don't know, maybe you'd like to fuck tonight?

Oh, boy. I was rolling. Jamal had to come over to see what I was laughing about. I almost–*almost* felt bad about it, but mind you this boy has been following my tail for almost a decade. I saw how embarrassed he was, so I told Jamal I was going on break. He looked at me like *oh shit*, and scurried off, but not too far. He was still within ear shot.

I quickly apologized to Chuck. I don't want any bad feelings between us, but that was a brazen move on his part.

I just told him that I'm not ready for that right now, but I'd be willing to hang out with him. He seemed relieved that I didn't rip into him any further, and quickly left the store without buying the teddy bear or the condoms. He didn't say much of anything, so I really wasn't a hundred percent sure how he was feeling.

Jamal came over and asked if I was okay. I said yeah and took the items back to their place and shoved the cart in with the others at the front of the store. I just don't know why he had to go and do something so stupid.

I was mad at him the whole rest of the day. Jamal and I talked as I restocked the carrots and lettuce, but at the end of my shift, he was off dealing with an angry customer as I mopped the floors.

Chuck walked in. I don't know how he knows when my shift is over, but *he knows*. I scurried to the back of the store and clocked out before he could get to me. I even left out the backdoor, dragging my bike with me, but he still somehow caught me in the parking lot. I almost rode around him, but he jumped in front of me. I slammed the brakes and hopped off my bike.

Getting right in his face I asked what the fuck his problem was. That's when I saw he had been crying.

Why I care, I don't know, but I instantly backed off and hushed my voice.

He told me his plans had been ruined. Chuck had wanted to come to my place, apologize, and invite me over since Joel wouldn't be back until tomorrow morning. He would give me the teddy bear at his place, and we could hang out. He *says* he didn't plan on having sex, only wanted to *prepare* for anything.

He just wanted to have a nice evening with me after thoroughly apologizing for being so careless and thoughtless.

Should I believe him?

Well.

I did. After the sniveling apology and explanation in the parking lot. We went our separate ways. He was to come over in an hour, giving me enough time to shower and decompress. After Chuck's ordeal in the store, two bottles of juice had exploded on me, so I felt like a sticky mess.

My parents wouldn't be home until around six, so we had time to watch a movie. I turned on the local news while I got dressed and waited for him to show up. There was a feeling of apprehension brewing in my gut, and I couldn't tell if it was because Chuck was coming over or because I was waiting to hear if another body was discovered.

Puppies. Puppies. *Puppies.* That's all the two babbling news anchors could talk about. I wondered if the segment would ever end when Chuck knocked on the door. I knew it was him because he always did the *Shave and a haircut, ten cents,* knock. As I walked to the door, the back of my mind itched. Was Chuck really capable of beating somebody up? I mean, he had hit Slim, but that was when he thought he was connected to Adam's death. *Maybe he's racist,* my mind whispered. A more plausible idea was jealousy, but anything's possible.

But in all honesty, I don't think he's capable of extreme violence. He's been a crier for as long as I've known him.

So, I opened the door, dumb thoughts twirling around in my mind, and I was met with a bouquet of flowers. Chuck shoved them at me before pushing his way past into the living room. I really didn't know what to say, so I said nothing, setting them on the kitchen counter and asking what he wanted to watch.

He was acting odd, standing all stiff and fidgeting with his phone. I took this for nervousness, but I'm still not entirely sure what it was all about. I asked if he wanted popcorn after making some. He declined. I asked if he wanted soda after opening one for myself. He declined. I even offered to watch a movie I thought he'd like, and he declined, stating he'd like to watch something I would enjoy.

I like horror movies, and I know Chuck does *not* have the stomach for gore, so I asked for him to pick instead.

Halfway through my bag of popcorn, we finally agreed on a movie. I had relaxed back into the couch, not happy with the movie choice but happy that something had been picked. We got to a scene where the main character meets the girl he thinks he's going to marry, and there it was.

Chuck's arm on my shoulder.

You know, I had sat over a foot away from him, just to set some boundaries with him. I thought some were already set in the store, but again, here we are. Somehow, he had squirmed his way over and snaked his arm around my shoulders.

No one has done that in a while, and I gave in. I leaned close to him, hoping he would keep it this simple. You don't realize how much physical touch matters until you hole up in your room for months. I felt like crying.

In a universe where Adam was still alive, I would have *never* done this, but because–because I'm hurting… I guess I needed someone.

I need someone.

Halfway through the movie, my parents barged in. I guess we had spent too much time arguing over what to watch. Chuck quickly retracted his arm and slid to the end of the couch as my mom flicked the light on.

I wasn't embarrassed. In fact, I was entertained. I know my parents have been waiting for this moment since Chuck's existence in our lives, and I know Chuck is a bashful bastard. I was able to disconnect from the situation and enjoy it as Chuck's face ripened to a cherry red.

My dad smiled and laughed, greeting Chuck. He always called him Chucky, something none of us kids called him. If he grew out his hair longer, I could definitely see him starring in his own horror movie.

My dad pretty much told Chuck to beat it in the politest way possible. I was almost mad, but then Dad said he had reservations at a sushi restaurant in Yuba City.

Sushi?

I've only had sushi two times in my life, and they were for very special occasions. I had to wonder what this special occasion was.

So, Chuck left with a bowed head, but not before giving my father a glance that was definitely hard to stomach. I gave him a brief hug before he left, but Chuck felt cold.

Dad and I loaded up in our van, but Mom stayed behind. When I asked why she didn't want to come with, he simply said, "She's tired, hon."

Conversations with my dad always start off slow. I never know what mood he's in or what he wants to talk about, so I brought up work.

As I spoke about Jamal, I realized how many little details I was going to have to leave out. My mouth was moving as my brain was calculating what was safe to say and what I couldn't. I tried to stick to the fact that Jamal had lost a loved one as well, and he was a good manager, and thank God my dad changed the subject.

We had driven past a homeless camp set up on the sidewalk in front of the abandoned theatre on E Street. He shook his head, and said, "Adam was onto something."

I looked from the shopping cart and tent encampment back to my dad, waiting for him to continue.

"He knew what the real problems were out here. He saw it all." He shook his head, saying, "All these people that drive by and do nothing. Say nothing. They have *no idea* what it's like."

Tears welled up in his eyes, and soon mine were flooded. Substance abuse has affected our area drastically, increasing crime, the homeless population, and the overdose deaths.

Adam knew it all because he *was* it all. He knew where to pull the problem from its roots. Part of me wants to follow in his footsteps, but would I be overstepping? I know he kept a notebook with ideas. Ideas on how to help people like him. Flaws he saw in the justice system and in the rehabilitation centers he had been to. He could relate to these people, meanwhile I feel like someone preaching from the outside of the church. I have no credibility. I can only work from what he's left behind.

I think my dad feels the same, having never struggled the way Adam did. You begin to feel useless or like you're a bad person. Having to tell Adam that he had a problem was always the hardest, especially once he became an adult. He was an adult making his own decisions about his own body. Who was I to say he was doing wrong? It may be illegal, but he was only harming himself.

The statement I loathed was, "I can get clean anytime I want."

While I wish it were true, it's simply not, but as a concerned loved one, you're only berated for the things you say out of love.

"I want you to quit," isn't an example of control. It shows someone cares.

"You have a problem," isn't to make you feel guilty, but only to open your eyes to the damage you're doing to yourself.

I was glad when we pulled up in front of the sushi place. It not only broke the silence, but also kept my mind from draining into sewage.

"So, Chuck, huh?" Dad asked as soon as we were seated.

I had to laugh. There was no way I was getting out of explaining this one. So, I kept the conversation light. Work this. Chuck and I are just friends that, and then he hit me with,

"Where's Adam's gun, Abby?"

His usual honey-brown eyes had turned into cold, dark pits as he asked. My heart fell into an abyss as my mind went to the gun hidden in that tree at Star Bend. I wanted to lie. I wanted to say I didn't know where it was, but he knew. He knew very well.

Instead of answering, I said, "Why?"

His eyes widened, and I saw him thinking. He asked, "Why do you need it?"

I thought back to the dead bodies, the USB, Joel, the pills, Ricardo, Detective Bill, Jamal's eye and slashed tires, the two men Chantelle saw the night before Adam was found, the grinding of metal through flesh, and a linoleum floor that would never really be clean. I thought about all the times Adam had brandished the weapon while we were out. All out of need for protection and never brazenness, but didn't that make it worse? I thought about Chantelle's baby and who would protect her and the child. I heard Adam beg for his life, bargaining that he would have the money they needed so desperately. I felt the gun's weight in the pocket of my cargo pants as I walked down the street, and as I became more comfortable with it over a period of days, it sat heavily in my waistband. Like a teddy bear to a child, that weight signified safety in my mind. Images rolled by of a life I was living in secret, repeating my brother's deadly mistake.

Over two sushi rolls and an appetizer, I told my dad everything.

Chapter Nine: Purpose

Recorded The Night of October 29th

My dad was appalled but not surprised. After I confessed everything from Joel's suspicious behavior to Chantelle's pregnancy, we sat in silence. Only the bustling kitchen and few quiet conversations in the booths around us could be heard.

It felt like I had vomited onto the table, and nothing was done about it. We just sat there staring at it, expressionless.

The food was to die for, but I could have lived without the awkwardness.

Now, of course we got home, and my dad immediately took my mom into their room to talk. I sat outside for a while, watching traffic roll by as the sun set. Were they crying? They were obviously concerned, but all I could do was sit on the porch and wish for a joint.

So, today my mother wanted to occupy some of my time. She insisted we go out thrifting and garage saling. I was a bit frustrated, having wanted to spend my free day roaming around the trees of Star Bend looking for dead bodies and retrieving the gun I almost prayed was still there, but I guess that's not what normal girls do, huh? So, I dressed in a flowery blouse and tagged along as my mother haggled over ceramics and paintings she would never hang. First, we hit the local garage sales, cruising in our ugly van. It wouldn't be so ugly if it weren't for the rust all over the hood and roof, but apparently the paint was defective from the factory.

I found a few old paperbacks and a skull ring that caught my eye, but when mom saw the ring, she gave me the *put it back* look, so there I left it. From there, we headed to Plumas Lake. My mother heard the whole neighborhood was doing a garage sale event.

Only in the suburbs.

She could talk for hours if I let her, so I was sure to cut her off every now and then. We met a woman who bakes from her kitchen, a couple that have a public gym out of their garage, and another couple with enough kids to fill a classroom. Then we met *Marvin*. Ah, I've met a lot of Super Mart greeters that look just like Marvin.

Grey, swooped over hair and thin rimmed glasses. He was selling a lot of crap that didn't make sense for an old man to have. A dollhouse. A wardrobe of dresses. Most startling was the two-foot stack of *girly* magazines sitting next to said dollhouse. But then I saw it.

A printing camera.

It was no name brand, but was anything I owned?

The answer is no.

I tried not to look too interested, but that's when my mom butted in with "*Ooh that looks so cool!*" You'd think years of her doing this would get her used to looking uninterested before buying the greatest thing you've ever owned.

Jeez.

So, the guy told us the price. I told him my price. He said no and offered to throw in a whole box of printing sheets plus a new box of pens that I could use to write on the photos. I said yeah, gave him his money, and left.

His genial charm of a Super Mart greeter had quickly worn off, and I realized he was just another creep.

The thrift store was fun. It's always interesting to see the things people are so willing to give away, considering the thrift store here only takes donations.

I was really just focused on what I was going to do once we left. I planned on skipping out on my parents and riding my bike to Star Bend. Again, I should really get a car.

By the time we got to the clothing section of the thrift store, my mom started acting nervous. She was wringing her hands around themselves and keeping quiet. I was just going to ask what the deal was when she blurted it out.

"Your father and I are worried about you."

Oh, how only eight words could send the iciest shiver down my spine.

I really am taking Adam's place. Those words have always been reserved for *him*. I didn't know what to say, so I said nothing. She didn't say anything else either, and I realized my parent's silence means they're disappointed in me.

What started out as an innocent curiosity has sullied into a dangerous obsession.

At least in their eyes.

I don't plan on stopping any time soon, but I may have to *pretend.*

So, that's what I did. We got home, I helped Mom unload the van, and I put on my old gym sweatshirt, a beanie, and my workout leggings. Then to top it all off, I pulled my hair back into the shortest ponytail known to man.

"I'll be out for a bike ride," I told her, filling up my water canister. She seemed to smile just a little and told me to be careful. I rolled out, with my new camera in my bag of course.

The ride over is always nice. It takes about an hour, and the cars drive by like they're trying to kill you, but in these moments of silence between the raging drivers, you get to feel like you're in another time. Me riding my bike past farmhouse after farmhouse could have happened twenty years ago, fifty years ago, or as far back as when the first bike was created. It's peaceful as long as my mind doesn't wander too far from the present.

There was a time when my brother would scare me with stories. He wouldn't tell me directly because he knew I'd snitch, but he would tell his friends about them right in front of me.

The one-eyed fish man. The three-armed pig farmer.

Yada yada, all that kid stuff. But even though it was dumb, it would still frighten me, most of all on these long bike rides. I would think about pedaling real slow to catch my breath, and a hand reaching over from a bush and snatching me off my bike. I couldn't think about what would happen next because I'd always pedal faster.

And now here I am frolicking in the forest with dead bodies and chasing a killer.

[silence]

Maybe my parents should be concerned.

By the time I got to the entrance for Star Bend, I was winded. I hopped off my bike and stomped my way up the steep driveway in hopes that the hidden parking lot would be empty.

I was wrong.

Ten or more cars and pickups sat in the lot. Luckily, most of the visitors were down by the dock, loading their small boats into the murky water or already out on the fast-moving mud. The Feather River isn't much to swim in as it'll carry your body out to Sacramento faster than you can say *drowning victim*, not to mention the water is so brown you wonder if it's sewage runoff.

Despite the heat radiating from my body, I kept my sweatshirt and beanie on. I didn't recognize any of the cars in the lot, but I really *didn't want to*. This was a solo mission and *God forbid* I run into someone like Chuck.

Speaking of, I haven't heard from him since yesterday. He didn't even text me to let me know he got home safe, but he did leave me on read when I asked if he was okay, so my guess is he's *fine*.

As I pulled my bike onto the path, the one that's not really a path but has enough space to walk, I looked down, realizing how meager my tires looked. I hoped to not blow one of them out, but also couldn't afford losing my bike. In hindsight, locking it up in the parking lot would have been the better solution. I was quick to ignore the new *No Trespassing* sign, figuring I wasn't the only one.

It wasn't long before I was hidden away in the trees. The boaters' screams and music had subsided and only the crunching of leaves accompanied me. I rolled my bike up to a tree and left it there as I explored the surrounding thirty feet. I felt so calm, something I can't feel in my apartment anymore. Something I haven't been able to feel in a long time.

I was near the place Adam's body was dumped, the place we spent so much time together. I have to wonder if he was there. I know I don't *believe* in an afterlife or God or spirits, but the mind still wanders. Could he have seen me looking for those that had been tortured like him? Was he proud of me for making a stand, or at least trying to?

I was just so calm.

Again, I thought of all the missed opportunities. The way he'd never hold his child or see his bride walk down the aisle. The way we'd never walk that forest again.

Well—

I don't know. I didn't feel his presence, but I did? If that makes sense. I felt whole again walking amongst the low hanging tree branches. Whole and calm and serene. The silence encapsulated me, and I felt every breath and every beat of my heart. The air was clean and didn't stink of cigarette smoke or weed.

I walked along, getting closer to Adam's stump. I could just make out the squiggles of letters carved into the side of it when my serenity was broken.

A deep sorrow replaced it as I gazed upon a young man. The sound of machinery ate at the back of my mind, reminding me that I had sat at a desk and listened to that for a whole day. I had walked the floors that Adam's blood had been spilled upon, talked amongst the men who had killed him, smiled and laughed and shed tears in front of them.

And for all I know, Joel could have helped.

I pulled out my camera and clicked a photo of him. I would need a lot of practice with this thing. He was only half in the photo, but it caught all that was needed. Pulling out a pen, I thought about Adam and Sola and now this unknown man. I didn't recognize him, so I simply marked his photo *Number 3*.

A chill crept up onto the back of my neck, so I moved on. There were others to be found.

I saw the tree I had stashed Adam's gun in and climbed it quickly. I was up twenty feet in the air before I knew it, and instead of looking down to scout more bodies, I simply reached my hand in the hidey hole, snatched the gun, and jumped down. I had sailed down at this height before, but the feeling was a little different with a loaded pistol in my hands.

I should have used the vantage point, but I was just glad his gun was still there.

I circled the area three more times before moving my bike further down the path. Three dead bodies.

That means two other families just as affected as mine is. Just as torn and broken and downright unfixable. There's no cure for death.

Feet stuck out onto the path, and I wondered if maybe I had stumbled across a homeless person sleeping. I mean, who would dump a body right off a pathway?

I was wrong.

This person was much farther gone than the others, so much so that it elicited a small gasp from me. Something had eaten their face off, leaving behind two rotted, unrecognizable eyes in a browning skull. What the killers had left behind, the animals had gotten to. Their body had bloomed into a carcass blossom, their empty ribs acting as petals that reached to the sky. The once red of their innards had rotted, leaving behind black stains in the dirt and on the fallen leaves. I could imagine that some of the nearby wildlife was still marked with this dark blood.

This body could have been left by anyone, but who else could be dumping bodies here? This question raised the hairs on the back of my neck as I stared through the lens at it.

Click.

I marked this photo as *Number Four* as I don't think anyone but a forensic scientist could identify this body.

It all felt like a dream. Although I felt fear, I was still calm. Calm and moving as though I was on stroll and not cadaver hunting. The bodies were frightening, but so far gone that I didn't think much of them. It was like staring at a skeleton in biology class. The most frightening part was thinking of the USB footage, thinking of what had been done to these people.

The next body was only feet from the last, and much, *much* fresher.

In fact, catching eye contact with it made me jump right out of my calm demeanor. For half a second, I believed I was staring at a live person. In that moment, I imagined holding her hand as I called an ambulance and watching her bleed out, helpless to stop it. Her head had been propped up against a tree, and her body lay before her, a bloody mess. I approached slowly, fearing I may hear her heart beating, or God forbid, see it.

The woman was lying still, and, upon closer inspection, not a glimmer of life was left in her eyes. What life may have been here when she was dumped was gone.

She was someone's daughter, someone's friend, someone's *everything* for all I know. So, I photographed her, gave her a number, and tucked her away with the others.

Something had to be done.

Seeing a girl so close in age with myself spooked me. I could be her. I could be any of these bodies.

I searched the area for hours. By the eighteenth body, I realized the sun was setting.

A whole stack of photos sat in my bag. I wondered what I was going to do with them. Hoard them? Hang them up in my room? Maybe hang them somewhere public to raise awareness?

Then *boom*. It hit me.

If I took them to the department, someone other than Detective Bill would see the problem.

And then something would have to be done about it. That calm feeling returned to me, almost as if to say I was doing the right thing.

I grabbed my bike and raced down the path, hoping, shit, almost *praying*, that the caravan of drunken people would be gone.

They were.

I hopped on my bike and forced it up the levee, then coasted down. My front wheel felt wobbly, and as soon as I could safely look down, I noticed a huge burr sticking out of one of my bald tires. The multi-mile ride back to town was sure to be *something*, I thought.

The sky turned that hue that makes everything around you pink. I always wonder if that's only something people in rural northern California towns experience, not that I've really been elsewhere.

I sped by the walnut and almond orchards. Their white painted bases flashed by in the dusk. It was getting *real* dark out, and I was only about halfway home. I was surprised that I didn't receive a single text or call from my parents.

The chill set in. I only noticed as my quick breaths puffed a white cloud before my face. Cars rode by much too close to me for my liking. I had to wonder if this would be my last bike ride. My last *anything*.

The bike tire weeble-wobbled side to side as I pushed harder. I was sure the rim would be entirely *fucked* by the time I got home.

I almost missed the split in the road by the time I reached it. I had no lights on the front of my bike, or anywhere at all, and the sun had fully set by the time I reached town. I swerved, bracing to be hit by a car, and thankful none was there to sweep me off my bike.

I don't like being out at night. Not because the tweakers, and not because the thieves, but because you never know what to expect. A stray bullet could pass through my spleen at any moment. A car with a drunk driver behind the wheel could grind me into the asphalt, never to see justice. A firework could be set off from someone's backyard and land in my hoodie to burn me to bits.

I just *never* know what's going to happen, and that's *terrifying*.

Luckily, I made it home okay. The rim of my tire was *bent*, but I was not. I walked up the stairs to my apartment with my bike before remembering I needed to drop off the photos.

I left my bike chained up by the front door. In case you're wondering, my dad found an old boat anchor and convinced his friends to haul it up the stairs so my brother and I would have somewhere to chain our bikes in the small outdoor hallway. It weighed more than most thieves out here, so we never had issues.

How's that for a fun fact?

I sprinted back down the stairs, somehow not surrounded by the dusk smokers that usually sit out on the balcony at this time of night. I guess it was too cold.

The police department is only a few blocks from my house. I figured I could make it there and back in a good amount of time, especially if I ran.

The thing about the weather in Olivehurst is, it's just as unpredictable as the people at night. Rain clouds had swept into the night sky like silent killers, and soon fat drops were landing on my hoodie. I hoped they wouldn't get to the photos or camera in my bag as I clutched it to my chest and ran like my life depended on it.

I definitely got my cardio in this week.

There, in front of the police department, I caught my breath. The fluorescent lights casted a white glow over the damp sidewalk as I struggled to retrieve the photos from my bag, no doubt bending some. I had my beanie pulled down to my eyebrows and my hoodie tightened over my face to where only my eyes peeked through. The chill was getting to me as rainwater seeped into my clothes. I trembled, entering the front office where I quickly threw the photos onto the desk and ran.

I had no plan when I came into the department, but my mind said *run!*

So run I did even as the desk clerk hollered after me. My feet stamped down the sidewalk as my bag thumped at my side. I thought about the sorrow I would feel if I came home and my camera was busted, so I clutched the satchel to my chest again.

The night bore down on me as I soared through the darkness only broken by the eye shattering light of the sporadically placed streetlamps. I felt its weight on my back, and I knew I had to get home. There were tweakers and thieves and killers and cops out here, all of which I didn't want anything to do with. I just wanted to be home. To be in my bed.

And I'm so thankful I made it home.

After catching my breath on the stairs and lingering out on the balcony for a while, I opened the door to see my parents and Chuck on my couch. Tears stained each of their faces.

A single thought crossed my mind.

Who died now?

"Oh, Abigail!" my mother cried out.

Was it me? Did they think I died?

As the three grasped me in an awkward group hug, I realized *my phone was on silent.*

Apparently, Chuck came by to see if I was home, only to be told by my worried parents that they couldn't get ahold of me. After the group hug was over, I was brutally scolded. My mother even wagged her finger at me as she yelled. They were disappointed in me but grateful I was home. When they asked where I had been, I didn't know what to tell them.

So, I lied.

I'm not usually a huge liar. If anything, I was only apt to follow Adam in his lies.

Adam. I'm doing all this for Adam.

I told them my bike tire went flat miles from home, which was true, but I nudged the truth by saying I was all the way out in Plumas Lake, biking to clear my mind. This way my mother couldn't say I was being reckless. I *was* biking in the suburbs at least. I told them I had tried to bike home and showed them the bent rim. I lied, saying it was like dragging a ton of bricks behind me with the bent wheel, so I had to walk all the way home. My father seemed to soften, but my mother was still angry that I didn't answer my phone. I told her I had left it on silent and was so involved in my own thoughts that I didn't even think to check it.

And through all of this, I felt this mounting tension, especially since Chuck was there. I used this, crying in front of them to show how stricken with grief I was.

Do I still grieve for Adam?

Yes.

But will I let it be a stopping block in my life?

No.

It's sad to say that it took my brother's death for me to finally find my purpose, but I've never felt more alive. I've never felt so much emotion. I'm so close to exposing the killer.

I'm *right there.*

You may be wondering why I've put so much detail into this audio diary, and the truth is:

I have no one else to tell.

I can't worry my parents with every little detail as I find it. I'm sure me opening up to my father was enough stress to last them a lifetime. And Chuck. Chuck is weird. I don't fully trust him as of now.

He left after I explained myself, relieved I was home but exhausted from *work*. I still don't know what he does.

I *have* to say all this to someone because if I don't, would it even be worth doing? Would all of this effort and energy be worth it if no one knew? I don't want fame. I don't want glory. Shit, I don't even know if I really want anyone to *ever* listen to these recordings, but if by chance someone does, I want them to know that life is possible. Even after loss. Even after grief. One can still find purpose.

[pause]

One can still find purpose.

Chapter Ten: Serial Killer

I was on the news, and *not* for finding my brother's killer.

Eating a bowl of cereal and drinking my coffee, the news anchor spoke haunting words.

"Serial killer appears to have dropped off photos of their crimes at the police station late last night."

Serial killer?

My eyes flicked up to look at the screen.

Me. That's ME.

Surveillance footage showed me squirming in the drizzling rain, prying photos from my bag, then entering the office and quickly darting out. The anchor continued on that the unknown person is now the biggest suspect in a ring of sudden murders.

Sudden?!

It's only sudden now that it's newsworthy. Tell some of those decayed bodies how *sudden* their deaths were.

With my parents in the back of the apartment, and away from the TV, I listened intently.

While the suspect dropped off gruesome photos of the crimes, they were not labeled with a location. Police can only work with what's in the background of the pictures and possible fingerprints on the photos.

A location?

[sigh]

A fucking location.

The news quickly switched over to a lighthearted story about the local pet store, so I switched the TV off. After scarfing down my cereal, I ran to my room, scooped up last night's still damp clothing out of my hamper, and stuffed them deep into the back of my closet. Anyone could have shown up in dark leggings and a dark hoodie, but I didn't need any more fingers pointed at me.

With a flat front bike tire, a bent rim, and the nerves of a rat in a cat shelter, I realized I'd have to go back to Star Bend. I figured a handwritten note or calling in wouldn't be enough. I would have to photograph another body and label it Star Bend, Olivehurst.

And if the fucking police couldn't figure it out at that point, then I'd go back out, take another photo, and label it with the GPS coordinates. I'd be sure to get the latitude and longitude a hundred percent correct.

I dressed quickly, opting for a pair of jeans and a sweater before I decided sweatpants and a sweatshirt would conceal my identity better.

I told my parents I was going to Chantelle's. I'm still surprised that they haven't asked to meet the carrier of their grandchild. It was only a day ago that they found out about her, but I thought they'd be ecstatic. The only reason I kept it a secret from them was for Chantelle's privacy. Maybe they were dealing with the same form of grief I was, knowing Adam would never get to see his child.

And I really was going to Chantelle's. The only part they didn't know was I was going to bum a ride to Star Bend.

As I was going to leave, my mother made a strange statement.

"I really think you should see a doctor, Abigail."

A doctor? For me?

I looked at her, stunned. The door sat halfway open in my hand.

"*A doctor?*"

She nodded, pulling away from me. "Your father and I think it would be best, so–" she paused, looking to my father who was standing in the kitchen. "So, I scheduled an appointment with a local counselor first. It's–it's for all of us to go. *Together.*"

I shook my head. I was, well, I was angry. How dare she think she knows what is best for my mental health. How I grieve is perfectly acceptable. Just because they've decided to hole up in the house and do nothing but dote on the police's every nonexistent word doesn't mean that's what works for *me!*

[pause]

I'm sorry. It's been a *day*. I'm just happy to be in bed, staring at the ceiling, and *alive*.

I waved her off, staving off my fury. I would store it in the place that held the drive to find Adam's killer. She let me leave, but not without a stern look of *you're-going-to-go-or-else*.

I didn't have anyone besides my parents at the moment. Adam's death signified a break from everyone I thought I could trust, not to mention the loss of Adam himself.

A funny thought made me smirk as I bolted down the stairs.

Ah, to live with a prostitute would make for a fantastical writing career.

But a doctor of all things. Not a hug. Not a shoulder to cry on. A fucking doctor.

Anyway, I made it to Chantelle's on foot without someone approaching me for money. I texted her prior, but she didn't respond. All I could hope for was that she was home.

I did have Chuck though. I could ask him for a ride, but even though he does have a beat-up car, I rarely see him drive it. Plus, the thought of a day in the forest with Chuck made me queasy.

She answered! I was ecstatic. I gave her a hug once she let me in and I could just see the baby bump. I refrained from touching it, but, dear God, I would give anything to see this baby. Would it have Adam's bright blue eyes? Or smile crookedly like him, my father, and I did?

I gave her the gift I had picked up on my shift at Super Mart. It was cheesy, but I hoped she would like it.

It was a mug that said, *"Best Mom Ever,"* in glittery pink letters. I thought it matched her apartment well, and she seemed to like it. There were no men present, and she was dressed in comfy clothes, quite similar to mine actually.

Fiddling with the mug, she blurted out, "I quit hooking."

My face sort of fell slack as I didn't know what the proper response was. Should I be happy for her? Or sad that she's quit her profession?

She continued on so I didn't have to respond.

"And I've been sober since I found out."

I smiled. "I'm proud of you, Chantelle." She really does care.

I found out that I could be comfortable in her presence and even in her apartment. So comfortable that we ended up crying again. I don't need a doctor. I need comfort.

We watched some TV together after crying and ended up eating popcorn even though it was too early in the morning for it. When the third episode was over, I asked her if we could go to Star Bend. She asked why I would want to go there, the remains of our tearful conversation still on her face. I told her about dropping off the photos. She was stunned to find out more bodies were out there. I omitted the part about being a potential suspect in the murder and was thankful to find out she hadn't seen the news this morning.

As I stood up to leave with her, she said, "Just take my car, and bring it back in one piece."

I cringed. "Chantelle, I don't have a driver's license."

She looked at me sideways. "*Girl*," she said, standing up. "How old are you?"

"Just turned twenty," I said, feeling my shoulders rise up to my ears.

She snatched her keys off the counter, and we left.

At this time in the morning, it's mostly young families unsuccessfully fishing off the incredibly steep banks that fall into the fast moving, muddy water. Only two cars sat in the parking lot, so I told Chantelle, "If I don't come back in twenty minutes, *don't* call my phone. Just *leave*." She seemed frightened by the command, but I had not only her life, but now a baby's life to think of. Before I left, I also said, "And if I call your phone. Don't answer the first time. Wait and listen to the voicemail. I'll say *pink glittery mug* if I'm in need of help and alone. I *will not* call if someone is after me." This statement got her eyes wide as saucers. She began to chew her thumbnail as she drove off to park.

I raced into the forest, running down the same path I had taken yesterday. I just needed *one* photo of a body. I twisted and turned and winded down further into the trees until I stumbled across a *fresh* one. I snapped a photo and turned to leave as my camera printed when I heard something.

Someone.

Two men were hauling something large behind me.

A body.

Just out in the open. No body bag. No garbage bags. Just a freshly shredded cadaver.

I threw myself behind a bush, hoping they hadn't seen me. I sat there in wet leaves and waited as they approached closer. My heart beat heavy in my chest.

Camera in hand, I realized I had an opportunity. Raising the camera's eye to my own, I focused in on the two dumpers. I couldn't see their faces, not yet at least, so I waited and waited. They waddled along, half carrying, half dragging the body between themselves. When I could finally see two faces. I pressed the button.

Click. Sssshhhh.

The two looked up, catching sight of me. I gasped, stuffing my camera and the photo into my bag before running. I bolted, straying from the path to follow a sparsely cleared secondary path. No one used it, so trees and bushes had grown smack in the middle of it, but I knew where it led.

They followed after, their footsteps thundering behind me. The weight of Adam's pistol sat heavy at my butt crack. *It was either them or me.*

I reached back, snatching the gun from my waistline and charged it. There was a fork in the path only feet from me. I grinded to a halt, sliding in the leaves and stumbling behind a tree. Firing once. Twice. Three times. I was shooting blindly as they came from a densely vegetated area. On the fourth shot, I heard a scream. I ran, veering to the right of the fork.

Diving around branches and brandishing Adam's pistol, I wondered how far behind me they were. I swerved around trees and launched over bushes in hopes to just *get to the road.*

Soaring over a patch of what I hoped wasn't poison ivy, I landed in an empty field. Plowed dirt lay out for acres ahead of me.

I felt like that deer in that movie. *Never enter the open field.*

But did I have any other options?

Not really.

I ran out into the field. The dirt was dry and crunched under my shoes. Any other time I would have savored each *crunch*, but, hey, it was *crunch time.*

Ha.

So, I cut diagonally toward the road, and I saw her.

Chantelle was driving alongside the road, the only thing separating us was a stretch of field, a field fence, and a drainage ditch.

This woman must be psychic.

I ran faster, pumping my arms like it would give me any sort of boost, and as I got closer and she slowed down, I could see her wide eyes moving up and down, following the gun in my hands. Like a track star, I hurdled over the field fence then jumped over the drainage ditch. I heard screaming from the forest as I slid around the hood of her car and jumped into the passenger seat. Before I could even speak, she floored it, sending me back. We were back at the parking lot in front of her apartment before any words were spoken.

"*Are you okay?*" Chantelle asked.

Her eyes stayed the same size the entire time, and she was panting and shaking in the driver's seat.

I looked down at the small bump of her stomach and realized what I was doing to her is wrong. I could make her miscarry my brother's child. I think that would send my parents, Chantelle, and me into a spiraling depression that would most likely lead in a quadruple suicide.

I didn't realize how much weight this child already bore in this world until that moment. I just hope she's right, and that it really is Adam's.

I told her I was okay, and looked down, shocked to see the gun still gripped in my hand. I slid it into my waistline as I exited her car. She asked if I would come inside with her. She said it would make her feel better to know I was somewhere safe.

So, we went inside. I sat down on her couch, wondering how many customers she'd had on it. I tried to push that thought away as I checked my phone. Nothing from my parents, surprisingly, but Chuck had messaged five times and called twice. He was desperate to hang out. I texted him back, letting him know I was at a friend's. That was sure to surprise him. I think everyone in town knows I have no friends. Well, I didn't. Joel texted and my stomach sank. I was supposed to be at work, not shooting at his coworkers in the guise of a chilly runner. I didn't answer his, "Where are you?" text, instead staring out the window as Chantelle busied herself in the kitchen. I hoped, well, I still hope that the men didn't get a good look at me. I feel like I'm no longer in the lion's den.

I'm in the lion's mouth.

Chantelle made coffee, and when she handed me my mug, she made it a point that I saw she was using the mug I gave her.

As she sat down, she said, "Mine is decaf by the way," as if I would know what that meant. I assume it's a pregnancy thing?

She asked me what happened, so I told her, and I came to the conclusion that how I told the story made me out to be quite the vigilante. I showed her the picture of the men, sure to cover up the dead body with my fingers. When she tried to pry my fingers away, I glared at her and shook my head. I didn't even tell her about the other photo.

In all honesty, this body had frightened me because it resembled Chantelle. Young, dark skin, long curls. I was thankful her eyes were closed as I stared through the camera at her.

Who was she?

A more important question is:

Will her killer ever feel the maw of justice?

We talked about a lot, and she brought up some great points that had slipped by me.

Why had Adam been missing for three weeks?

This was something that had crossed my mind but was stored very deep, like under a pile of blankets in my head. We tried to come up with theories. Chantelle's made the most sense.

If Adam owed a debt, she said it was most likely they would work him until it was "paid."

Three weeks of working for a drug gang and then a merciless death. I felt sorry for Adam. I felt sorry for all of them.

She also questioned how so many bodies were being dumped but not reported by anyone. To counter that, I told her how the news had been lying about low crime rates. I know the police know. At the very least, Detective Bill knows, but I think more cops are on the payroll of this drug gang. I also told her in recent weeks they had put up huge no trespassing signs all around the forested area of Star Bend. She made a statement that gave me chills.

"Almost as if the county has roped that area off as a designated dumping ground for these motherfuckers."

Oh, I could believe it.

Anymore, it was rare I saw anyone in the tree line beyond the asphalt parking lot.

Free labor.

Free dumping ground.

Well, it came at the price of paying off however many officers, but I believe it was about more than money.

Money makes people greedy, but power makes people insane.

And someone who kills people in such a fashion and dumps their bodies like worthless waste has to be insane.

Chantelle asked me what I was doing for Halloween after a period of brief silence. The holiday hadn't crossed my mind, not that it did in past years. Holidays were Adam's thing, especially Halloween. I think his best costume was when we were eight, and he dressed up as Benjamin Franklin. This was a period when my parents still had hope that he would follow his dreams of becoming a historian.

That was truly what the child version of Adam wanted to pursue.

I, on the other hand, refused to dress up. I've never been an attention seeker, or really an attention grabber. Adam was meant for the spotlight.

Sometimes the grief still gets in the way of what I know needs to be done.

I told her I didn't have any plans, and she looked at me like I was crazy. She had plans to put on a mask and scare the kids who came to her door before giving them their treat.

I thought it was nice she had plans and still celebrated the holiday. I'm sure my parents would be hunched on the couch, thinking of past Halloweens.

When she got up to use the restroom, I felt it was my time to leave. So, as she closed her bathroom door, I called to tell her I had to leave. I said goodbye and quickly left the apartment.

It started to feel stuffy and cramped. I'd been bouncing my knee so much that I caught Chantelle staring at it multiple times.

I really just didn't have any more words to say, and the pictures were burning a hole in my bag. I had to get them over to the department.

The day was grey and cold, and I wondered how kids would want to run around in this in thick costumes and cardboard. Was candy really worth it?

I was nervous. I was so nervous I could feel my core trembling. Would they have security out front? Or would there be officers in the front office waiting for me? Would I not be fast enough and get snatched up before I get out the door?

All these things were swimming around my mind, and before I knew it I was in front of the police department.

It was like *bam*.

People walked by. Cars drove by on the street. I even spotted a few officers chatting it up out front. No one seemed to have an eye on me, so I slipped in.

There's a wall of brochures on one side of the room. I acted as if I was glancing through them.

Oh, yes, I'm definitely interested in this volunteer program. Oh, maybe I could donate some of my time to *this* organization.

By the grace of God, or whatever I as an atheist should be saying, the clerk wasn't at the counter. I whipped out the photos and set them on the counter before taking a last look at them.

I forgot the fucking location.

I scrambled for a pen, finally finding one under a newspaper on the counter. The clerk's footsteps approached from another room back behind the counter. I scribbled on the white strip of the photo, but the pen wouldn't mark any ink.

My heart raced in my chest.

What would they do if I got caught?

I'm their biggest suspect right now.

I threw the pen aside, accidentally tossing it to the ground behind the counter. Digging in my bag, I found a worthy pen. Thank you, Marvin. I scratched *Star Bend* onto both photos and turned to leave.

"Oh, how can I help you?" the clerk called. She sounded nice, but her voice made my stomach knot up.

I raced outside, and as I threw myself out of the building, from the open door, I heard her scream.

Running, running, *running*.

People looked at me strangely as I passed, well, I assume that they did. I could see nothing but a blur. I even ran up the stairs of my apartment, only taking a few minutes to calm myself before entering.

There they were sitting on the couch. The room was dark, only a sliver of grey light filtering in from the barely parted curtains. Not a light was on. The TV was black. They were just staring forward.

I asked if they were okay, and they answered like nothing was wrong. Like I didn't just walk in on them while their minds were in another realm.

I wonder if they think of a life where I died instead of Adam.

I don't have the gall to ask.

So, I sat on the couch and turned on the TV. I assume they haven't seen the news, or if they did it didn't click that their daughter is the biggest suspect in her own brother's murder and the murder of God knows how many others.

Chuck texted over and over and over. I told him I was busy with my parents, and as I was typing, I got a text from Jamal asking if I'd like to come in for a late shift tomorrow. Since I had no other plans, I didn't mind.

My parents seem to be lost. I don't understand how they're sitting so idle. The police haven't been in contact with us other than the contact I've made with them. It's heartbreaking to see them so lifeless.

Bringing the killer to justice will never bring Adam back, but I'm hoping it'll give me and my family a sense of safety.

Chapter Eleven: Halloween

Chuck begged me to hang out, so I obliged. He told me to meet him at the park, the one we've been going to since we were kids. I felt more comfortable there than I did back at his place, considering I'm avoiding Joel.

When I walked to the park the sky was grey, but by the time I slipped under the awning covering the picnic tables, it was drizzling. Chuck was already there, a stupid grin on his face. He gave me a much too tight hug, and we sat down. I tried to ask about his job, but he didn't seem too keen on talking about it. I hadn't seen anything on the news about the suspected serial killer, aka me. I know I wrote the correct place down, everyone calls that place Star Bend. I think it's even on the sign, but I've been by so many times I don't even register it anymore. I heard the clerk scream. That must mean she saw the photos.

The rain pitter-pattered on the metal awning. It was calming. I'm not going to lie. I sat on the table, resting my feet on the seat, as I always do. Chuck sat on the seat below me and kept inching closer to my leg. I kept my knees together, tight, uncomfortable at the possibilities. I think he noticed this, or he was curious what I was looking at on my phone, so he scooted off the seat and plopped down onto the table next to me.

I kept checking local news websites, in hopes that something would be posted. In hopes that if something was posted, somebody else could come forward with more information, condemning Adam's murderers.

I think I checked every five minutes. It was really all I could think about. Chuck's words sort of droned in the background of my mind, the forefront taken over by everything else.

Finally, Chuck said, "Who are you texting?"

Jesus, he irks me.

I told him no one, but when I checked my phone after five minutes passed, he asked again. I asked him why. His eyebrows scrunched down. He said no reason, that he was just curious. Yeah, okay.

I made up my mind that if he put his arm around me today, I would not allow it. I did not expect what he actually did.

There was a period of silence as both of us watched the rain dump on the playground. It thundered on the awning above us, like a hundred marching band drummers. It was so quick. I couldn't have stopped it if I tried.

He grabbed my cheek and turned my face towards him before kissing me.

I think he expected a romantic moment, us kissing while the sound of rain orchestrated around us.

It did not go that way.

I pulled away, wiping my mouth with my sleeve quickly.

"What is wrong with you?" I asked.

He looked stunned, before the anger set in. "What is wrong with me? What is wrong with you?"

Me? Oh, I don't know maybe that my brother was brutally murdered, and I witnessed it, on a USB I found. Oh, and at his funeral, I dropped his fucking cat in the grave and his own coffin crushed the fucking thing to death. Ah, and my parents are in a deep state of grief, so far into it that even I, their only living child, can't help them.

I didn't say any of this. I just tried to calm him down. My excuses being:

"I'm not ready for a relationship. I'm still healing."

That only made him angrier. He hopped off the table and got in my face, saying, "You've been leading me on this whole time." His face was bright red with anger.

I just shook my head. Yeah, asking a friend for comfort in a time of need, in a time of grief, is clearly an attempt to lead said friend on romantically.

I never would have agreed to hang out these few times had I known he'd react this way. Without Adam here, I guess Chuck feels empowered. He feels that there isn't a barrier between him and I anymore.

So, I have to become that barrier.

I turned to leave. He grabbed my arm. The weight of my pistol, yes, mine. It's no longer Adam's. He gifted it to me. It's mine now. The weight of it sat heavy on my waistline. Could I do it?

If he gave me enough reason.

I yanked my arm away and walked out into the rain. I didn't look back, but I didn't hear his heavy footfalls behind me either.

On my walk back to my place, I realized most kids' Halloween would be over by the time I got to work. Ten p.m. was a long ways away.

When I got home, I fell into bed. My mom didn't question it as she knew I was going to be working late. I slept the deepest sleep I've slept in a long time.

Surprisingly, I woke up thirty minutes before work. Just enough time to get the crap off my face and start my walk to work. I told my mom goodbye, and she told me Dad was stuck working late. As a local mechanic, that happened often, especially with the junkers the people here bring in.

I took the only umbrella we own and started what felt like the longest walk I've ever taken. It was dark, and I hate walking at night, but there I was, fighting the wind and rain to go stock some carrots and celery. By the time I got to work, my jacket was soaked. I stripped it off and threw it in my locker, hoping it would dry by morning. The night was off to a good start.

Jamal greeted me, nice and dry and warm from his car's heater and heated seats, not to mention the nice metal roof he got to sit under. In that moment, I would have licked the bottom of his shoe just to sit in a warm car for five minutes.

He noticed my gloomy countenance, and surprisingly asked what was wrong instead of assuming it was simply the bad weather putting me in this bad mood.

Instead of just complaining about the weather, I felt comfortable enough to open up. As I mopped the produce section, and he changed out the empty plastic bag rolls for big, fat ones, I told him about Chuck.

"So, you've known this boy a long time?" he asked.

"Sadly, yes," I answered, watching a mysterious red stain get soaked up into the mop.

He shook his head. "Oh, no. Don't let him get to you. He's just sour."

Yeah, now that I think about it, Chuck did taste kind of sour.

I told Jamal how I couldn't believe Chuck was so quick to make a move on me. He told me that's just how some guys are. They're blinded by their own needs. All kinds of people can be that way.

I think that's true. And honestly, that statement has me wondering a few things. Am I blinded by what I want? Are my parents struggling because of what I think of as my needs?

I wish I could just let it all go, but I have a feeling I'm so close.

Jamal told me to go on a walk around the store with him. He needed to see what all needed to be done across departments. I followed, carrying his clipboard and marking things here, writing a note there.

We passed the candy aisle, and I saw Jamal do a double take. A few steps later, he said, "Why don't you go finish up the job Bella was supposed to do?"

He walked me back to the candy aisle and pointed to a cart full of bags of candy. "Those bags accidentally got left in the back. All I need you to do is put them on the shelf in the right place." He was smiling oddly, but I shrugged my shoulders, gave him the clipboard, and walked down the aisle.

There was someone in costume looking at the big bags of chocolate. It was a guy. He was wearing one of those spandex skeleton costumes and when he turned, I saw his face was painted with jarringly white and black paint.

Even under the paint, I noticed he was cute. Ah, the guilt I felt. Just having told Chuck I wasn't ready for a relationship and seeing this guy that made my heart flutter. Was I a hypocrite? I don't think so. But I really did hope this guy would talk to me.

There I was, my stunted, black ponytail still damp with rainwater and matted down on my forehead, and this guy says,

"So, your costume is a beautiful girl working in a place she deserves to never have to see again?"

Longest. Pick-up. Line. Ever.

But it worked!

I thought for a minute, trying to come up with something to say back. So, I said, "And your costume must represent the stock market?"

As soon as the words left my mouth, I wondered why I said it. What the fuck is wrong with me? I didn't think he'd laugh or even smirk at the stupid joke.

He laughed! It wasn't like bend-over-and-slap-your-knee laugh, but it was still cute.

Ugh, I really shouldn't be gushing like this, but who else can I tell? I think it's too soon to tell my parents or Chantelle, and Chuck, well, he just wouldn't be happy for me. For obvious reasons.

He asked me what kind of candy he should get for his brother. I guess the kid is sick and can't go trick or treating, so he, his name is Lenny by the way. What a dorky name for such a cute guy. So, Lenny is getting a bag of candy for his brother. He told the kid he would go trick or treating for him, but Lenny thought this would be quicker.

I told him he couldn't go wrong with a bag of chocolate candies, as long as the kid doesn't have a nut allergy. He snagged a bag from off the shelf and thanked me for helping him. He said, "I don't have much to offer in return for your help, but here's my number." He took the pen from behind my ear and gently grabbed my arm, scribbling his digits onto my wrist. Lenny laughed and said, "Just don't wash your arm until you text me." And when he winked, he said, "I'm Lenny Leniston." I said my name, and of course he asked if I ever play the drums. I laughed and said no as if I'd never heard the joke before. He told me he had to go and made sure to tell me to text him when I got off work. I told him I would.

He walked down the aisle, and I'm not going to lie, I watched him go, but that's when I saw him.

There Chuck stood at the end of the aisle. He glared at Lenny as he passed, having to look up at someone for once as Lenny is even taller than him. I sensed that he'd been standing there for a while. Long enough to at least know Lenny hit on me.

I didn't feel safe. He flicked his gaze to me, staring deep into my soul. I made a run for it. I speed walked down the aisle, and as I went, I heard Chuck's shoes squeak on the linoleum as he followed me.

I sped up, not wanting to run through the store. Oh, to have seen Jamal, or any other co-worker for that matter. Shit, I would have taken the company of any customer, but it seemed as if the store was vacant save for me and Chuck.

I just had to get to the break room. The front exit was actually closer, but the idea of being out in the dark parking lot with Chuck terrified me. I weaved through clothing racks trying to lose him. His wet shoes gave away his location as he neared me. My calves burned. I wasn't used to speed walking for this long. I wanted to break out in a full sprint, to make it to the break room and lock myself in the employee bathroom. There had to be *somebody* else in this store, I thought.

I came across no one.

Those silver doors shone in the fluorescent lights like beacons of safety. Seeing no one else around, I ran, closing the distance between me and the doors, and threw myself onto them, practically falling into the break room.

Jamal sat at a table looking relaxed while staring at his phone with his legs crossed comfortably. He looked up at me with wide eyes, prepared to ask what was wrong when Chuck busted through the doors.

Immediately Jamal was on his feet and yelling. He got between me and Chuck, pushing me back away from the doors. Chuck was surprised, obvious by the stunned look on his face, but when he saw me, he tried to push past Jamal.

I never saw Jamal as the violent type, but when he bared his teeth and shoved Chuck with both hands, I knew he saw me as a daughter that needed protecting.

Chuck fell out the doors, and from the sounds of it, landed on his back. I couldn't see from behind Jamal. He was yelling at Chuck at the top of his lungs, and security rushed over. I approached the doors, watching as they dragged him out.

Jamal made sure I was okay, his demeanor instantly returning to the man I know. We sat down and talked about it over some coffee, and he told me he would stick with me all shift.

"Do you have a lift?" he asked as we walked back out on the floor.

I shook my head. "No, and my bike is broken."

"I'll take you home," he said, giving me a one-armed hug around the shoulders.

The store was definitely more fun away from the produce aisle. I followed Jamal around, and we finished up his checklist. It felt kind of nice to be walking around with the head honcho.

We had lunch. Well, the kind of lunch you have at two in the morning. He asked me how stocking the candy went before Chuck showed up. I knew he did it on purpose. So, I showed him my arm and said, "His name is Lenny."

He laughed and told me he had a feeling it would work. He also told me I need to stay away from boys like Chuck, because he's exactly that. Just a boy. And boys don't know how to treat women.

It was rare to meet someone so blunt, so candid, but I thoroughly enjoyed his company.

I was replacing garbage bags in the cans around the store, and when I got to the front of Super Mart, I saw Chuck was staring through the front windows. I didn't want to act scared as we held eye contact. I wanted to appear strong, but I was shaking in my boots. Well, I was in tennis shoes, but you know the phrase. I looked away, putting a bag in the can and wrapping the edge over. When I looked up, he was gone.

Jamal came over and asked how I was doing, startling me. When I jumped, he jumped, and I felt bad. I told him it was just nerves.

The hours seemed to pass like slugs on concrete. I'd never worked a late shift, and I don't think I would ever do it again.

I was sitting in a chair at the closed sandwich shop, practically falling asleep, when Jamal told me it was time to go. I felt guilty but I could see the pity and understanding in his eyes. He led me to the back of the store, saying he didn't want to leave out the front. I agreed.

Walking through the parking lot felt like a scene in a horror movie where the music is building and growing louder, and you know the killer is right around the corner, but the character can't seem to figure it out. The parking lot's lights only illuminated circles directly below their bulbs. There was plenty of pitch-black space.

Jamal got into a little blue car. It had brand new tires, since his last set were slashed, and a sticker of the state of Texas on the back window. When I got in, I saw on the dash that he indeed did have heated seats. I don't think I've ever punched a button so fast.

He turned on the radio, tuning it to a country music station, and backed out of the parking space.

The sense of relief I felt leaving that parking lot was immense. As if I'd lost fifty pounds within a second. Jamal asked me where to go, and I guided him to my apartment. When we got halfway there, I realized Chuck could be there, waiting. Jamal must have read my mind as he said he would get out and walk me to my door. He asked if my parents would be home, and I told him they should be. My dad was working late, but he should have been home.

He pulled up, parked, and walked me to my door without an issue. But when I opened my door, all the lights were on.

My mom was in the kitchen on the phone. She was crying. Jamal saw this and decided to invite himself in with me.

She saw me and walked over silently. She was listening to a voice I could barely hear on the phone. With trembling hands, she gave me a hug. My stomach was filled with lead. I wanted to ask where Dad was, but I was scared.

Was I prepared for the answer?

"Your father is in the hospital," my mother said, pressing her cell phone to her chest as she said it.

Jamal and I gasped.

I asked if he was all right, but my mom held up a finger, listening. She hung up shortly after, sat Jamal and I down without even asking who this stranger was. She took my hands in hers and said, "We're going to visit him, but we have to be strong. The doctor says he's *very* hurt."

I nodded. An anxious feeling built up in my gut, so similar to the feeling I had when two, then three, then four nights had passed without Adam.

She looked at Jamal and asked if he'd like to come with. He shook his head. I could understand why he wouldn't want to come with. So, we went outside, only to discover our van's tires had been slashed. It was Mom's day with the hunk of junk as they took turns carpooling. Jamal overheard my mother cry out and ran over from his car.

He offered to drive us to the hospital, and my mother thanked him. It was rare to see her take any sort of help, but I'm glad she took Jamal's.

The sun wouldn't be rising for a few more hours as we drove over the river. My mother was completely silent, and I tried to think about what she'd be thinking about. Probably money.

Not in a selfish way. I'm sure her first priority was my father, but I had overheard them talking about the cost of Adam's funeral. Funerals aren't cheap. Hospital bills aren't cheap. And without any knowledge of what injuries my father had sustained, I was clueless to know how bad life was about to get.

I hate hospitals. I think that's a common feeling for most people. Hospitals are really only there after bad things happen.

Jamal stayed in the car while my mother and I poured out into the rain. I thanked him on my way out, noticing how he averted his eyes from the hospital building. I had to wonder if his daughter had made it to a hospital, with everyone hoping she would survive, only to die in a bed.

I can't imagine how many people have died in this hospital.

We rushed in, catching the eyes of the receptionist and the surprisingly full waiting room. Apparently, the receptionist had been the one on the phone with my mom when I got home. She directed us to go down the hall and to the left. As we walked down the hall, I noticed how close his room was to the emergency entrance. It must have been bad.

Tubes and wires snaked around my father's face and body. Bloody gauze constricted him from moving. His closed eyes told me he wouldn't be moving for a while anyway. The room clicked and beeped over the sound of the heating duct above my head.

It was bad.

Chapter Twelve: Fear

The bruising was the worst. His eyes were swollen shut, and the doctors told us one of his eye sockets had been broken in three places. It had been a blunt object that caused these wounds. I'm sure the stab wounds were much worse than the bruising, but thankfully I was kept from seeing those. By the time we got to the hospital, they treated those.

There were five. Technically four and a slash wound. One in his chest. Two above his left hip. And one just below his armpit that went through the muscle of his chest and out. Thankfully so or worse would have been done. The slash wound went from his collarbone diagonally across his chest, slicing his nipple in half.

One of his legs had been broken. It had been busted at the knee. The doctor said he would never walk the same again. That is, if they could get his kneecap to heal properly.

He had lost a lot of blood, so much so that they required a transfusion. He wasn't conscious for this decision, so the doctors chose to do so.

When work was over, my father was to meet his co-worker in the parking lot so they could drive home. Like I said before they do this every other day. When twenty minutes passed, his co-worker assumed he might have been busy or in the bathroom. When forty minutes passed, he grew concerned. He went back into the shop and checked my dad's office. He checked the shop floor. He checked the waiting room. He was nowhere to be found. So, the last place being the lot where they stored customers' cars behind the shop, his co-worker went outside.

My father was laid face down on the asphalt in a puddle of his own blood. His co-worker quickly called police.

I learned all this this morning while visiting the hospital. His co-worker, a man who goes by Teddy, came to see him and explained everything. The police had shown up, asking us questions like who had he been in contact with lately, and did he recently have a falling out with anyone?

We answered, but I kept things short. One of the officers that came in was the younger guy that had come to tell us Adam had been found dead. He hadn't been in contact since that day. I really didn't have contact with any of them. Nothing more had been done about Adam's case.

It was a rough day. Doctors told us my dad was in a coma. They hoped it would be short, and they thought with his injuries that it should be. But I wasn't so sure.

I was skeptical of everyone. If the police wouldn't help me, why would a doctor help my father? This began to pour out into other parts of my life. I noticed when I went to the convenience store this afternoon, I wondered why the clerk would bag my things. They were my things, why was he helping? Why did the person in front of me let me go ahead? They didn't have to do that.

We weren't allowed to stay overnight, so we came in at the earliest time we could, which was late in the morning since we had to wait for someone to come change our tires. My mother stayed all day, but the room was so cramped and humid that I had to get out.

I walked home, much to my mother's discontent. It was only a walk over the river and two or three miles to get to our apartment complex. When I got home, I took off my jacket, seeing the phone number.

Lenny.

I completely forgot to text him. I hoped he didn't think I stood him up, so instead of sending him a text that could easily be ignored, I called him.

He picked up after a few rings but didn't say anything when he answered. I said hi and introduced myself: and he seemed gleeful that I called.

When he asked why I didn't text him once I got off work, I didn't know if I should tell him. He said he was worried all day since he had expected a text early that morning. I asked if he was really that worried, and he said yes, that he was worried I didn't like him and the guy he had seen leaving the store weirded him out. He had contemplated sticking around to be sure that the creep didn't do anything to me, but figured it was just his over imaginative mind.

I told him I knew the guy. That the guy is obsessed with me and chased me through the store after he left.

He apologized profusely, and I told him not to worry. It was then I decided I should just be honest.

I told him that I didn't text him because my father was in the hospital. He had been beaten into a coma.

Silence.

Then he took a deep breath and apologized. I don't think there's another response for when someone gives you such painful news, especially when you don't know the person very well.

He then asked if I'd like to go to dinner to get my mind off of things. It may sound sleazy, but he asked in a tone that signified he truly cared. It didn't sound like he was just looking for sex. I told him I don't have a car, and he said it was no problem, that he'd gladly pick me up. I asked where we were going, and he offered to take me to a Mexican restaurant down the street. I agreed, we set a time, and I told him I could actually walk there.

He said with an obsessive maniac on my tail he wouldn't let me walk anywhere and to text him the address as soon as possible.

I think I like Lenny.

I tried to find something nice to wear. I almost chose my black jeans and a black dress shirt, until I remember that's what I wore to Adam's funeral. When would I bring that up? If he asked what I did for fun, would I tell him I didn't do anything for fun? Would I tell him that my only focus in life has been solving the murder of my brother?

It was sure to be an interesting topic.

So, instead I chose a flowery, long sleeve top, something my mother had surely picked out for me five years ago, and a pair of dark blue jeans. I wouldn't be caught dead in my tennis shoes outside of work, so I pulled out an old pair of mock army boots I had from high school. I had to dust them off a little bit, but they looked nice.

My mom texted me to see if I was alright. I told her I was fine and going to dinner with a friend. I was sad I didn't get a chance to tell her I met a guy yet but sitting next to my father in a coma wasn't exactly the best place to do so.

I stepped outside, only to realize I would need a sweatshirt over my shirt. So much for looking colorful.

I waited out on the balcony for Lenny, wondering what he drove. It was drizzling outside and cold enough to see your breath, but I felt none of it. I didn't even feel that excited about the date. Rather, I almost dreaded it. I say almost because it was better than sitting alone in my dark apartment or in the dreary hospital room beside my barely surviving father.

Lenny showed up in a small pickup. I don't think I've ever seen one so small. He parked and met me at the bottom of the stairs, then took my hand and led me to his truck. He asked how my day was. I saw a flash of *I probably shouldn't have asked that* across his face.

I wanted to make him feel bad for no other reason than my life was shit. But why mess up the only good thing going for me?

So, I said things were going well and that I was just worried about my dad. I didn't say it sarcastically. I didn't add any extra tone or attitude. I just said it and asked how he was doing.

He opened the door for me, and the cab of his truck didn't reek of cigarettes or pot. I thought I could smell cinnamon.

Despite Lenny and I being close in age I don't remember ever seeing him around, then again it wasn't super common for a person to live in the same town their entire life.

He came from a town south of us, called Woodland. I distantly remember going there to look at houses when I was around seven. But even back then, houses were too expensive for my parents. When we had shown up to Woodland, I had been very disappointed that it in fact was not a woodland full of prancing deer and fairies, but a sad, agricultural town.

I asked why he chose to move somewhere like this, and he said his job had brought him out here.

Día De Los Muertos is a small restaurant. I usually just pick up food from the outside window. I don't think I'd ever been inside until going in with Lenny.

When we parked, he opened my door and grabbed my hand to help me out, and when we got to the restaurant, he opened the door for me again.

Either he was raised right or he's really trying to earn some brownie points.

We took a seat by the front window that overlooked a bustling, dirty street. The menu was daunting, especially for a person that doesn't like eating in front of people. Besides sushi, I think Mexican food is one of the worst foods to eat in front of somebody on a first date. But that's just coming from my paranoid brain. Tacos make you open your mouth all wide, and you have to hold your head sideways. Burritos, again, make you open your mouth wide, not to mention the farts later on. I would *never* plan a burrito date followed by cuddling and watching a movie. And nachos just get your fingers all dirty, and you have to sit there and either lick them off or scrub them with a napkin. And after all that work, they still feel sticky. I realize that that doesn't even touch on most Mexican cuisine, but that's about the only three items I usually get.

Alright, enough about the food. Food makes me nervous. At least in front of cute guys.

He chose to sit with his back to the window, so I got stuck watching traffic drive by in the rain behind his head.

It almost took precedence over what he said. He was talking about his parents, and all I could think was *red car, white truck, black truck, blue car, green SUV*, and so on and so on. I just hope there won't be a quiz about what we talked about today.

Our food arrived, and I picked up my fork and knife cautiously. I would eat this burrito with dignity, hold in any farts I may have in his car, and spend the night alone in my apartment. Movie dates were a bit much for a first date. Too much potential.

This time he was talking about something I can't remember while I tried to keep my eyes from the road. It was just light enough to see cars with their headlights on. The sun was setting behind the sea of grey clouds in the sky.

Joel's car drove by. My heart skipped a beat. I've been avoiding him for quite a few days now. I would have thought it was just a coincidence that he drove by the restaurant I was in, but then he drove by a second, then a third, then a fourth time. By the fifth time, I was sweating.

It's hard to avoid someone that knows where you live. It's hard to avoid someone you grew up with.

Fifteen minutes passed and I didn't see him again. By this time, we were almost finished with our dinner.

Lenny had gone silent, and I hadn't noticed. I apologized and decided to at least partially come clean. I hope it would help him forgive me for being so absent on this date.

He already knew my father was in the hospital, but he didn't know the extent of everything else. I briefly explained that my brother had recently been murdered, and that I really could think of nothing but it for weeks. That is, until my father.

His eyes softened, and he looked to be on the verge of tears. It was rare to see someone show so much sympathy; someone with a bit of empathy.

He asked how I was handling it so well, and I was taken aback. *Handling it so well?* I guess in his eyes I was a hard-working girl with a sociable side. He hasn't seen the darker, isolated person I really am.

Maybe he saw a glimpse of it through my tired eyes on that date.

He ordered dessert and offered to split it with me since I had declined when the waitress asked. I declined his offer as well. I couldn't tell if it was the beans or the fact that Chuck drove by that made my stomach turn. Again, it would have been of no importance had it been once. But no, it had been over and over and over as Lenny happily scooped up his flan and ate it.

"You sure you don't want some?" he asked as Chuck's car crept by. He asked a second time before I said no.

He apologized about my current situation. It warmed my heart a little bit, if I'm going to be honest. I tried to tear my eyes away from the street to look at his face and maybe salvage this night. I told him to just start asking me questions, and that I would ask one in return for each of his. This always worked when getting to know someone when I was younger. I learned a few facts about him. Like he has a pet snake named Dragon, and he likes pumpkin pie all year round. I thought that was pretty weird, but quirky at least. Without jarring Halloween makeup on, he has a handsome face.

He asked if I ever had any pets. I cringed, stating we used to have a black cat. I told him that was a story for another time, a less depressing time. He nodded solemnly. I'm sure he was thinking I was still heartbroken that our cat had been run over or just never came home one night. The truth was just unbelievable.

By the end of the date, I felt less anxious. I couldn't tell if it was attributed to the fact that I was more comfortable with him, or because I hadn't seen Joel or Chuck drive by again. We packed up our leftovers and left the restaurant. The rain was pounding down, and in an adorable move of chivalry, Lenny took his jacket off and held it over my head as we ran to his car.

He held my hand on the drive home and had a light smile on his face. When we parked at my apartment complex, he looked over and said, "I'm glad I met you." I returned the phrase, feeling weird. I don't think anyone has ever said that to me, let alone a cute guy.

I keep saying cute because saying handsome over and over seems odd.

He got out, running around the front of his car and almost slipping just to open my door. He closed it and grabbed my hands.

He said, "I had fun tonight."

And just like in the movies, we kissed in the rain. Nothing extravagant, just a short lips meeting lips. No tongue.

My hair and face and shoulders were damp and cold, but inside I finally felt warm. I almost teared up thinking about

Adam. Weird to think about your brother when you're kissing somebody, right? But I thought about if he could see me right now, how much he'd make fun of me, and how much I would love it. How much I would trade the world for it. No price is too much. Adam could make fun of me every waking day for the rest of my life, and it'd be better than him being gone.

I was thankful for the rain, so Lenny couldn't see the tears running down my face. I wonder if he tasted their salt.

See if Adam would have been alive, I never would have been stocking those shelves at the job that he was supposed to have. I never would have met Jamal. I never would have met Lenny. I feel like I'm in Adam's place still. I mean, I'm sure things wouldn't exactly be the same. I'm sure Adam wouldn't be standing in the rain kissing Lenny, having met him on Halloween night. But maybe him and Chantelle could have had their moment if it had just been me six feet under instead of him.

He pulled away, staring deep into my eyes. I hoped he couldn't see the tears. He was smiling, so I'm sure he didn't.

We walked to the stairs to my apartment, and he said goodbye. I watched him run out of the rain and dive into his car. As he backed out of the space, I turned to go up the stairs, looking up to catch Chuck's blazing blue eyes from the balcony.

So, someone was indeed watching, but I was sure he wasn't going to make fun of me about it. No, he planned to do much worse.

Instead of getting theatrical with it by asking what he was doing at my apartment, I gave him no attention. Simply walking up the stairs and trying to walk past him. I don't know why I thought that would work. When his hand shot out and grabbed my arm, I didn't know how to feel. I knew I was supposed to be scared, but at the same time I was filled with rage. The audacity of this guy.

I shoved him off, figuring his first attempt would be light but his second attempt would be the kill. He wouldn't let go if I let him get me again. So, I ran.

I hit my door like a linebacker, so thankful that someone had left it unlocked. I didn't, but somebody did. I fell inside, actually slipping on the tiles by our front door, and jammed my shoulder into the ground. I'm sure our downstairs neighbor was curious as to what the fuck was going on. I looked up to see Chantelle and my mother looking at me with eyes the size of ostrich eggs.

I slammed the door shut with my foot, scrambling to stand. I stood up just in time to see Chuck barrel through the door. It swung open, almost nailing me in the side, and a wet, red-faced ginger stumbled in.

I latched onto the door, about to slam it into him, when I heard a very familiar *click*.

I saw Chuck freeze before I saw Chantelle. She stood there like a Charlie's angel. I watched in awe.

She said, "You've got about three seconds before I put six holes in your chest."

I don't believe Chuck has ever been faced with the barrel of a gun, but I do believe this isn't the first time Chantelle has pointed a gun at someone. All color left his face, and he backed away slowly, letting go of my arm. He closed the door, and, after I locked both locks, we watched out my parent's big, picture window to see if he would leave on the main road toward his own place. We had no windows facing the parking lot, and I was too scared to go outside. So, we waited.

A few tense minutes passed before he sped by in his beater.

I was still confused as to why Chantelle was in the apartment with my mom. One, I was surprised my mom was home and not by my father's side. Two, I was curious why and how Chantelle and my mom had gotten acquainted.

I learned as we watched reruns of an old cartoon that Chantelle came over looking for me. I guess she texted me, and I just hadn't noticed. I should probably take my phone off silent once in a while. It was already pretty late, but my mom made us all tea and heated up a TV dinner for her and Chantelle. I realized I left my leftovers in Lenny's car, and that's when I brought him up. We already discussed Chuck, and my father's condition, being the same as earlier when I was at the hospital, so I thought a little good news would cheer them up at least a little.

My mom was ecstatic, despite the dried tears on her face, and Chantelle asked all the questions.

Is he cute?

What does he drive?

Where does he work?

I didn't even think to ask him, so I texted him on the spot, telling him I had fun, again, and assuring him if we went on another date, I wouldn't be so spacey. My mom fell asleep in dad's recliner, something that broke my heart to see, and Chantelle fell asleep on the couch beside me.

I couldn't sleep. So, I've been here on my bed, retelling this odd day. Lenny finally responded about five minutes ago despite me having texted him two and a half hours ago.

He works at Soki.

Chapter Thirteen: The End

Recorded The Night of November 2nd

He's dead.

Lenny's dead.

They found him in his parent's backyard with a bullet hole in his head. Whizzed right through his brain. Shit, maybe the burning bullet touched a few memories of our first and only date.

Should I kill myself?

Is it me?

Every man around me is dying.

Adam's dead.

Jamal got his ass handed to him the night after meeting me.

My dad is in a coma from getting bludgeoned within an inch of his life.

And my first real boyfriend is dead.

That leaves Joel and *Chuck*.

They have to be responsible. It's just not possible for them not to be.

Joel came to my apartment today. He stopped by to see why I haven't been at work or responding to his texts and calls. I only opened the door as far as the safety chain would let me. Chantelle had gone back to her place this morning, and my mom was at the hospital. I was all alone, but my gun sat in the right pocket of my cargo pants. It seemed to buzz in my pocket, like a cellphone does while it's ringing. I could almost hear it say, *"Use me, Abby. Touch my barrel to his forehead and tickle my trigger."*

I didn't, but it was everything in me not to blurt everything out, to call him out as a killer and become one myself.

I told him I was sick and not responding to anyone. He cocked an eyebrow and asked why I was at work at Super Mart and on a date if I was so sick.

I knew someone had been following me, but it still made my heart stammer in my chest. He treated me as if I owed him something. He'd only ever been a bad friend to Adam, and now

I think he's the reason Adam's dead. I kept myself from trembling. I didn't want him to see how distraught his presence made me.

"Fine, you caught me. *I quit.*" I said, slamming the door shut. I let out a shaky sigh and sat in my dad's big, stretched out recliner with my knees curled to my chest. I watched the door, knowing damn well Joel could blow it down any minute or shoot me right through it.

He and Chuck had been talking. Or maybe Joel was following me separately.

Two stalkers?

Are two stalkers working separately better than two stalkers working together?

I think this all depends on if one stalker has been stalking me since a young age and the other has an entire drug gang's arsenal at his disposal.

Mom called.

My ringer scared *the shit* out of me.

I guess my dad mumbled. He didn't fully wake up, and he didn't say a full word, but he made noise. She was so excited.

I don't know.

I feel so disconnected from all this.

Like I'm staring in through a thick glass window, completely unaffected. I'm not the ant farm owner, but I'm an ant staring into the ant farm from under a shot glass. Confined. Alone. Tired.

What if he never wakes up? Do we keep him hooked up to fifty machines until we die?

How does that work? If Mom dies and I die while he's still unconscious, does the hospital just pull the plug?

I should be by his side, doting on him. I just can't. I can't sit in that hospital room. I can't smell all the chemicals and linens. I can't listen to the beeping of the machines and the buzzing of the fluorescent lights and the hum of the heater and the drip of his IV. I just can't.

I can't solve Adam's murder either. The police and media have done nothing with the photos I brought in. I've checked online hundreds of times in the last few days. Nothing. Not even another mention of a possible serial killer. All that work, almost dying, all for what?

There is no justice.

Adam will lay in the ground and rot. Star Bend will fill up with dead bodies, all people just like him. Detective Bill will continue to get paid, and the drug gang will continue to sell drugs to children and sick people on our streets.

Adam was going to be the change.

Now look at me. I was curled up on the damn recliner for at least two hours, trembling with my gun in my hands.

I walked to my room, and looking out my bedroom window at Smith's, I noticed someone looking in my window. He stood in dark clothing on the sidewalk right in front of the store. He had his arms crossed and a hat shading his face, so it was indiscernible. But he was staring right at me.

I snapped my blinds shut and sat on my bed. The apartment was quiet without my parents. While they were gone, I rarely ran the heater or AC, and it was too cold for fans to be on. Just flat silence.

Even my neighbors seemed to be quiet, and the cars out on the road drove by silently.

It all gave me so much room to think.

Where do I draw the line?

If I know who killed my brother for a fact, and I've tried my damnedest to get the police to do something about it, *who says I'm in the wrong if I do something about it?*

Thoughts of obtaining a machine gun and walking into Soki ran through my mind. I'd blow down Joel and Ricardo and Saul, saw them in half with bullets. Maybe I'd make Molotov cocktails and throw them through their windows. Yeah, find out where they live. Fuck their families. Look at my family, all torn apart and broken.

I thought about how I could obtain explosives. I'd be willing to die just to make sure it worked. Wear a vest with explosives all over it. And *boom*.

The place would be history.

No more nasty green pills for Joel. No more *nothing*.
[click]

I fell asleep and woke up with some sense. I need time to grieve.

All this time I've been avoiding emotion by attempting to solve this murder. We already know who did it. We should have known from the beginning. Adam was just in with the wrong crowd.

And now I feel like everyone around me is crumbling apart.

Waking up, I had to wonder if everything was connected. If who killed Adam was who killed Lenny, was who beat up Jamal, was who beat up my dad.

I just don't know why a drug gang would target those people in particular. My dad was not a customer. As far as I know Jamal and Lenny were not customers.

I wonder if this is how other families are feeling. With as many bodies as are rotting out at Star Bend, there's got to be families wondering where they are, too.

Everyday more missing persons posters are stapled to the telephone poles, are taped into the bus stops, are posted online, and I can tell you where half of them are going.

I'm just stuck.

I tried to eat lunch, heating up a TV dinner in the microwave. The macaroni and cheese was too wet and the meat was chewy. Doesn't really matter, I guess. You could have fed me filet mignon, and I would have hated it anyway.

Chuck called, like eleven times. By the last one, I finally picked up.

"What is wrong with you? Why have you been following me around?" I screamed into the phone.

Chuck was on the other end sniveling. He said, "I just heard your dad is in the hospital in a *coma*. How could you not tell me? I want to come see you."

I lied and said I wasn't home. He said he would meet me anyway, just tell him where to go and he would follow. God, he makes me sick. I told him I didn't want to hang out, that I was busy trying to figure some things out. He kept bugging and bugging and bugging until finally I snapped.

"Tell Joel this, too: *I never want to see you again. If you come back into my life, something bad is going to happen to you.*"

Click.

I'm shaking. I don't think I've ever been so furious in my life. Chuck is so demanding, and always has been. I could never see myself putting my need for attention before someone's feelings. I guess he just doesn't care.

I need to chill out. Just think about something other than the things that have been consuming my mind for weeks. I guess the present situation is a good place to start.

Do you think Dad will ever sit in this recliner again? It's really comfortable from his big butt wearing it down over the years. Feels like a giant, soft bowl.

[sigh]

I think I'm gonna go for a walk.

[click]

Something—something happened. I'm in a rush. This may be the last time I ever check in.

Chuck came over. I told him on the phone I didn't want to see him. I don't know what his problem is.

Was.

And he didn't so much as come over, as he did break in. I went to the gas station down the street to grab some candy. I guess I'm a depressed eater. When I got home, I talked to my mom on the phone for a while, watched TV and ate the candy, then got up to do the laundry. I was in our dining area, aka the small space between the living room and the bar of the kitchen, folding laundry and organizing them into their separate baskets. One for my mom. One for me. And this load of laundry didn't include any for my dad.

That's when I heard it.

Over laughter from the TV, I heard the faintest footstep. It was so light that I almost missed it, but there it was, only feet behind me.

I had set the gun down on the side table next to the recliner. I guess after eating some sour candy, I felt at ease enough to part with my gun.

That was a mistake.

I turned around, much to Chuck's surprise. He lunged at me as I lunged at him. Arms grappling each other, we tumbled to the floor, and with him being the size that he is, he easily pinned me.

"I have to tell you something," he whispered.

I asked him why he couldn't just text it to me or tell me on the phone. He told me he couldn't say it over the phone. I asked how he got into my apartment, and he said he didn't have time to answer that.

He spoke quickly.

Joel was on his way with a group of men.

They had plans to slaughter me.

I never felt my heart race as it did pinned under Chuck. I thought my wrists were going to snap as he used his full weight against me. I didn't believe him at first, mainly because of the crazy look in his eyes. They were glazed and extra wide, but the pupils were pinpoint small.

He breathed heavily in my face, almost panting. I thought of a rabid dog. Chuck said that they knew that I knew everything. I told him I didn't know everything. I didn't know anything about anything. All I knew was that Joel was working as a line worker at Soki.

They had footage of me stuffing a USB in my purse while I was in the bathroom.

I fucking knew it.

I told him I had taken some files off the internet and brought them home.

"*Liar. You're such a liar,*" he spat.

I asked if we could talk like rational people. He said we were talking like rational people.

We seemed to bounce back and forth like this, getting nowhere and wasting time like sitting ducks.

"Well, if they're on their way, why don't we leave?" I asked, interrupting a rant Chuck was on about how many guns Joel had.

"No. No, we can't leave," he said, scrambling off of me. He lifted me up by my shoulders to sit up and hugged me close. Should I have squirmed away then? Yes. Did I fear for my life? Also, yes.

He smelled of sour sweat and smoke, and heat radiated off of him like his insides were on fire.

Could Joel have gotten this simple pot smoker to try his pills? I thought so. It was a definite possibility.

I thought of the many times Adam came home sloppily high. Itching and scratching and talking really fast. I think people think that's something from the TV, but certain drugs make people so hyperactive that they can't control themselves.

Adam was a laid-back kid. He was rambunctious as any young boy would be, but there were always periods of long silence from him. Periods of introspection I believe. In his days of sobriety as an adult he would have these, and I think that's why he would ask me so many strange and dark questions.

Was there any truth in what Chuck was saying? Yeah, so I had probable cause to believe him. But why would he know such a thing? Why would he be clued in on what Joel did behind closed doors? So, I asked him:

"Why do you know all of this?"

Here his eyes shifted to wet, sad, puppy dog eyes.

His next words made my stomach drop.

"It all started with Adam."

Oh my God. Chuck was part of it all along. While he held me and cried with me, he knew more than I ever could. While he knew I was struggling for answers, he's had them the whole time.

Here's what I can recollect:

Joel began selling for Ricardo. Ricardo works for Saul.

All of this I knew, but not without having worked hard for the answers. Chuck could just spew all this out like it was nothing. There he sat on my dining room floor like we were hanging out on a Saturday night.

Joel got Chuck into the business. Chuck was a cleaning boy. *He helped mop the blood and dump the bodies.*

All for some green pieces of paper.

Joel also got Adam into the business, but in a different way. *Adam was his customer.*

Joel was giving away their new product, *Sour.* Well, in the beginning at least. After a week or two of providing this new drug, he cinched up on his customers. When they couldn't pay, but begged for the product, Joel gave in, most times partying with them.

Ricardo was looking for his money, and when his golden boy had no explanation for where the product and the money was, his head was on the chopping block.

Joel constructed a whole scheme to get free labor, but Saul turned it into a sick game. Joel would bring in the people who weren't paying, tell them they were headed to a party or something, then knock them unconscious.

They would wake up, almost entirely nude in a room full of tables covered in powder and presses. A guard would tell them, "*Get to work,*" with a rifle aimed at their chest.

Chuck knew all this because he would come in sometimes to clean up after the ones who resisted.

Joel lured Adam to Soki with the promise of another all-nighter. Adam woke up with a lump on the back of his head and worked *three weeks* for these men because he thought his life depended on it.

Saul pointed out that Joel hadn't thought this plan all the way through, and that they would have to execute all of the laborers. He decided to turn it into a game.

The man loves horror movies, so he disassembled a conveyor belt and strapped on a boat motor to it to make it run exceptionally fast. The exposed inner workings of the conveyor belt proved to saw right through people.

Just like the videos I watched.

Bodies were dumped right down the road at Star Bend, and most of the time it was Chuck and Joel doing the dumping, until Saul hired two new, bigger men. One of which had recently been shot in the leg.

I stood up, wanting to be as far away from Chuck as possible. I asked, "Were you there?"

He nodded, solemnly.

I felt no pity for him as I crept closer to the side table by my dad's recliner.

Chuck was crying. Fat tears rolled down his cheeks, and he said, "I didn't want Adam to die, but it was either him or me and Joel."

I said, "*I wish it would have been you and Joel.*"

He looked up at me, hurt. "No, don't say that, Abby. Oh, Abby, we've gotten so close since your brother died."

A spear was thrown through my heart. The dots were slowly connecting.

"Did you–"

His words were mumbled, but I could hear them loud and clear, "*Then other people started getting in the way of us. They had to be **removed**.*"

He continued on as I listened intently.

"I felt so close to you after Adam died. Like that barrier between us was finally broken, finally *gone*. I felt that I could help you in this time of need. Then you started working and talking about *Jamal*." A sick smile crossed his face, and he shook his head. "Stupid motherfucker didn't even know it was coming." He laughed. It was a cold, distant laugh.

I stood there, stunned.

Out of all my notions, I never believed Chuck was present for Adam's murder. It killed me that it was Joel. Adam's best friend turned drug dealer turned killer. If it hadn't been the conveyor belt of doom that got him, it would have been their new drug *sour*.

Before Chuck could continue, I asked, "What does sour do?"

His eyes lit up. Maybe his cleaning job wasn't *just* for green pieces of paper. "Like Cloud Nine itself, baby."

I've never understood what that phrase refers to, but he moved on.

"You know how pills are usually super bitter when they get stuck in your mouth? Well, this one's sour, like candy. I could eat twenty, thirty of them, but they'd kill me before I got that far." He laughed. "You get all twisted in reality. One minute you're just chilling, next minute there's a penguin sitting on the couch next to you! Then, the real high starts. Pot has always given me a good high, but sour is like that times a *million*. I don't really know what I'm doing during that period, but it's usually so short that I can't get into much." His demeanor seemed to loosen as he drooped his shoulders down, almost pouting.

"What are the downs like?" I asked.

His eyes snapped up to mine. He said, "Like the worst hell you've ever been through."

"Where are you?"

"I just took one before I got here." His face contorted into a tight smile.

I nodded. I was only a foot away from the side table at that point.

"Yeah, Abby, but when I'm with you the high is always there," he said.

What a sick fuck.

He smiled wider, saying, "That's why I beat your dad and killed your boyfriend."

I killed him.

The gun felt so right in my hands as I aimed it at Chuck's nose and pulled the trigger. The bullet careened through his forehead, a red wave of blood and brain matter spraying down the wall behind him.

He fell limp onto the floor, and here I stand in my bedroom, telling you all this.

In a flash, a life is gone. A spray of blood and brain matter signifies the death of a friend. Who am I to take a life and go unpunished? I bore the fatal consequences of Chuck and Joel's actions on my shoulders for *weeks*. I gifted him his own fatal consequences with a bullet to the head.

[distant gunshots]

As bullets fly through the parking lot of my apartment complex, and as I listen to the bloody screams of Saul's gang and the police, I leave you with this recording so justice can be found for the countless murders of Olivehurst.

Many lives were taken, and may the families find closure in the conviction of the killers, if that should ever happen. I hope this recording finds you well. I leave my phone on my bed and will surrender myself to the police and gang members surrounding my apartment complex.

With you, I leave my final words:

I love you, Adam.

Epilogue: The Aftermath

It's been three years since I've recorded this damned audio diary. I condemn it yet, it's the only thing that saved me from spending life in prison.

Upon leaving the apartment, I walked out into a shooting between police and Saul's gang. Apparently, Saul showed up to murder me himself, and, unrelated, someone called the police after they heard me and Chuck wrestling–I can't say who.

People just as dumb as me were out on the balcony watching, waiting for a stray bullet to lodge in our guts. I stood there, like Rose on the Titanic, and almost prayed for a bullet to spray through my brains, just like the one in Chuck's head–just like the one in Lenny's head.

I looked on as men killed each other just for showing up at the wrong time. Gleefully, I watched as the gang members struggled to keep up. I believe they had prepared to squash an ant, not swat at a hornet's nest. Woefully unprepared, these men took fire, cowering behind their cars. I watched them bleed out, screaming from the balcony as if I were at an old gladiator tournament.

When I screamed over the gunfire, Joel happened to be getting out of his car, ducking on the side of it. He heard me and looked up. We made brief eye contact before a bullet struck his face. It was a caliber so powerful that it blasted through both car doors before blowing out his cheeks.

In a spray of blood and teeth, Joel was laid flat on the ground. He convulsed on the asphalt. I pulled my bloodied pistol out from behind my back to the awe of my fellow onlookers and *aimed.*

Joel rolled onto his back and looked up at the sky, then to me. I squeezed the trigger, watching the bullet in slow motion as it careened for his forehead. He was thrown back like a ragdoll, lying flat on the asphalt as his brains splattered.

Best shot I've ever taken.

I was thankful my mother was doting at my father's side as all this went down. She would tell him everything was going to be okay and that he would make it out better and happier. She was wrong.

Oh, my dad pulled through. He's okay, just been stuck going to physical therapy every other day. Maybe one day he'll get all the feeling back in his legs.

I calmly went back into my apartment, leaving the front door open. I sat on my dad's recliner. A family ran by once, and I couldn't tell if they were running to their apartment or trying to escape. The little girl glanced in, and I hope to God she couldn't register what was lying on the floor.

Only a few minutes passed before the gunfire ceased. I heard the police make their orders, but I knew everyone was dead.

I remember it all like it just happened.

But.

The courtrooms.

They are all just a blur in my mind.

I know a police officer or two or three, I can't recall, came in and arrested me. They even checked Chuck for signs of life. Like I would let that bastard live.

At some point, they found my recordings. I can't remember if they were first used for me or against me in court, I just remember cringing at my voice. Eventually, they helped me, so I can't complain. I served two years in and out of prison before I was found *not guilty* by a jury of my peers. They tried to get me for murder and obstruction of justice and carrying an unlicensed gun, etc., etc.

My representation fought like hell, and I don't know why. I didn't talk the entire trial. I think that's what hindered my freedom. It's what made it all take so long. Not to mention, they had to pull the truth out of this web of lies the police and Saul's gang had constructed.

Detective Bill died in the shootout, so he was of no help, but the receipts for luxury items that came from untraceable money definitely helped my case.

As for the other bodies out in Star Bend, they were recovered. All seventy-four of them. It took a very long time, but they're at least in a morgue somewhere. Half haven't been identified and a quarter have so far been unidentifiable. That leaves nineteen families with the gruesome truth. I hope they can find the closure I still don't have.

As for Chantelle and the baby: little Adam was born while I was locked down. She video called me at least, so I got to see him. DNA proves him to be Adam's boy, and he is the only thing that brings me any happiness. He's got Adam's smile and his eyes. He's just got a little curlier hair and darker complexion. A perfect mix between the two.

My parents didn't want to live in the apartment anymore. I can't blame them. They've fallen in love with Junior so much that he and Chantelle live with us in a new town. It's still an apartment, but it's bigger, roomier, and far away from Olivehurst, and that's all I could hope for.

I don't know why I felt the need to say all this. I suppose I miss feeling like I have someone to talk to. A private ear to confess to. Somewhere to go when it all overflows in my mind.

There's been a lot of missing persons' posters showing up in this town. My heart sinks every time I see one. Where is Raul? And Charlotte? And Esther? And Whitney? And Justin?

Their bodies could be rotting just like Adam's was. What haunts me most is that Adam was one of the freshest bodies at Star Bend. Saul's games had been going on for *years*.

After all this time, I have to wonder, why was Adam's murder the first of seventy-four solved?

Indicted Fiction is an audio drama podcast diving into crime and horror. Season One follows *Adam's Murder*, so be sure to check it out if you'd like a read-along experience.

Listen for free on my YouTube channel @alyannapoe

MUKBANG

What happens when a twisted mukbang fan gets her hands on her favorite mukbang star?

MUKBANG: A Social Media Horror Story

When the world came to a halt in 2020, so did Jack and Mia's career.

Travel vlogs become a thing of the past, and Jack discovers a new, wetter, stinkier side of the internet:

MUKBANG

With no social contact during COVID, parasocial relationships soar, and as a fan of Jack's, Rochelle falls victim to a strange social media obsession, going head over heels for this new mukbanger. Meanwhile, Jack's wife, Mia, loses herself to isolation, abuse, and neglect. Her own OCD and intrusive thoughts make escaping into her mind impossible. Like a caged animal, she paces the house, biding her time…

Jack's newfound fame as a mukbanger gives him all the praise and affection he could ever want…

So where does that leave Mia?

And what will Rochelle do to get closer to her favorite content creator?

A comedic, splatterpunk slasher, MUKBANG is a dream for gross-out fans and an absolute nightmare for those with food aversions.

Available on Amazon

Get signed copies at AuthorAlyannaPoe.com

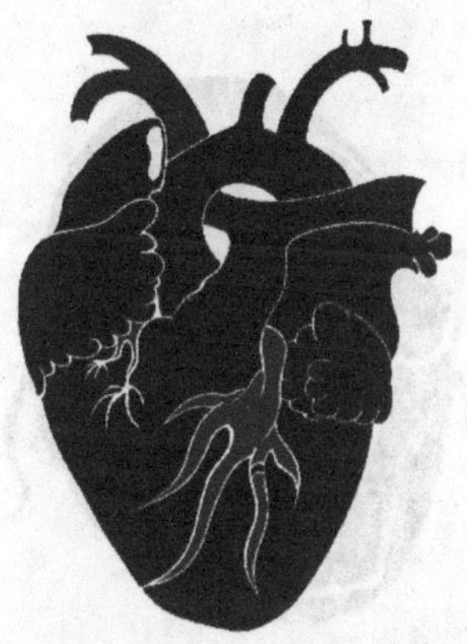

HOME

When Jeff saw her online ad for artwork…he knew he had to
have her.
The young beauty reminded him of a special someone, and he
just had to bring her
HOME
What happens when a young woman is forced into the vows of
a stranger's delusion?
HOME
With no way out, she is forced into a new life, and her old life
fades out of existence.
Until she sees a familiar face on the news.
Questions race through her mind.
"Who am I?"
"Am I–"
HOME
Welcome **HOME**, dear…dinner's on the table…
A dark thriller, **HOME** is a cautionary tale for all young
women out there…
You never know who you're going to meet…
And no one is going to help you…
Available on Amazon
Get signed copies at AuthorAlyannaPoe.com

NO GRACEFUL DEATH

21 bite sized tales of terror all wrapped into one horrific package.

What you'll find inside:

A haunting Halloween tradition carried on by a lone survivor.

After an argument with her husband, a woman escapes into the ocean on a small boat, only to be met with a fight she may not be able to win.

The power a vintage clown mask can hold within a couple's relationship.

A strange invisible extraterrestrial interrupts a couple on their tropical retreat.

A hateful husband exacts his darkest fantasies against his wife.

Discover these horrors and more in No Graceful Death: A Collection of Short Horror Stories. From gothic to splatterpunk to sci-fi horror, this collection has something for every horror fan.

Notice: This collection hosts previously published stories. Alyanna Poe's past collections Cradles the Brain and REJECTS have been consolidated and edited into this collection. Added to these stories is one exclusive story under the title A Stranger in Velvet.

Available on Amazon

Get signed copies at AuthorAlyannaPoe.com

Author Alyanna Poe studies cannibalism and fails at other art forms when not writing grotesque and sad stories.
She likes skateboarding, riding dirt bikes, and kickboxing.
But most of all, she likes connecting with readers through stories and videos.

If you enjoyed this book, and even if you didn't, please leave a review on places like Amazon, GoodReads, and your social media.

Find her online @AuthorAlyannaPoe or @AlyannaPoe

Thank you :))